Hearing Lies

Hearing Lies

OLIVIA SMIT

WhiteSpark

HEARING LIES
Copyright © 2021, Olivia Smit

WhiteSpark Publishing, a division of
WhiteFire Publishing
13607 Bedford Rd NE
Cumberland, MD 21502

ISBN: 978-1-941720-47-9 (paperback)
      978-1-941720-49-3 (hardcover)
      978-1-941720-48-6 (digital)

Praise for *Hearing Lies*

"*Hearing Lies* takes readers on a lyrical journey through the lives and hearts of two unforgettable siblings. Returning to Golden Sound for her sophomore novel, Smit weaves a story that is at once familiar and unpredictable. Falling into the pages of this story felt like coming home, and I never wanted to leave. The ending left me smiling in satisfaction and holding the book to my chest, wishing for more."

TAYLOR BENNETT, author of the Tradewinds Series

"Smit is the voice in contemporary YA fiction that I needed back in high school, and honestly fills in what I feel has been missing from many of the books in the genre. Her work is the essence of grit and hope, and she will most definitely be on my insta-buy for my future TBR. I don't care what the genre, whatever she writes, I want to read it."

HOPE BOLINGER, author of 12 books, including
the Blaze trilogy and Dear Hero duology

"Hearing Lies does what all good sequels do: it brings the seed of a story planted in the first novel (Seeing Voices) and brings it to full life under its own light. The cast has grown up a little bit between books, and the narrative voice is stronger for it. Olivia Smit masterfully allows the reader to grapple with guilt and redemption through the heart and mind of her characters. Even the fairly benign conflict of "saving" a local library presents a backdrop for relentless tension. We talk a lot about books having satisfying endings, and this one does in the sense that I felt myself mentally exhale in the final chapters."

ALLISON PITTMAN,
author of Pudge and Prejudice (Tyndale, 2021)

For Hannah and Zayya.
Hearing Lies would never have existed without you!

~

1 Chronicles 29:10-11

Chapter ONE

Skylar

Anastasia's moving
The library might close
Can you come?

I'VE BEEN STARING AT THE SAME THREE TEXTS ALL DAY, AND SO FAR, NOTHING'S changed. Cam's words from this morning are no less ominous than when I first read them in the dim light of my bedroom. I thought the morning sunshine, the normalcy of a late spring day spent studying for exams, would chase away the uneasy feeling in my belly, but so far, no good.

My own line of texts trails away after his, twelve different responses (all equally inadequate, some bordering on insensitive) all trying to fill the gap where everything okay is supposed to be.

Anastasia can't leave Golden Sound. The library can't close. What is a small town without its treasured inhabitants? What's summer without shelving books with my two favorite people?

"I need this," I whisper to myself, like it will make a difference. "Don't take this away from me."

Someone pokes my shoulder, and I flinch before I can stop myself, glancing up from my phone to find sunshine pouring in my bedroom window. I'm still not used to the random, out-of-the-blue taps and touches that make so much more sense when you can hear the footsteps or sniffles or even the sound of someone's clothing rubbing together. Instead, it's like being kicked in the dark at a sleepover. No warning. Instant pain.

Janie leans off the end of my bed, poking the back of my shoulder with her pencil. She's saying something, but I took my hearing aids out when she started playing music a half hour ago. I roll my desk chair out a little so I can reach the bottom drawer where I usually stash them, turning each one on before winding the plastic cord carefully around my earlobe.

Janie's voice leaps into my head mid-sentence, and I have to squeeze my eyes shut for a second to let my brain adjust.

"—party, and I said—"

"Sorry—" I hold up a hand like I'm directing traffic. Cam's texts still spin around in my head. "Can you start over?"

Janie's smile looks like it's stuck on at one corner, slipping half-heartedly off her face as she sucks in a deep breath. "I was just going to say," she starts, and then waits for me to nod before continuing. "If you want to come to the grad party, you can."

The end of her sentence, unspoken, rings loudly in my imagination. *Even though you're not graduating with the rest of us.* Even though my injury from eleventh grade has confined me to yet another semester stuck within the halls of our high school in the least-victorious thirteenth year ever taken. Even though my other friends are moving on.

"Thanks." I untie my hair and begin twisting it back into a braid. "Who's hosting again?" I won't remember. I won't attend. But they don't know that yet.

"Daria." Janie holds her phone out to me. "Skylar, you should totally come. We'll have fun."

I nod, pretending to be focused on the end of my braid so I won't have to look her in the eyes. Will we have fun? Or *would* we have had fun, if everything was the same as it used to be?

"Skylar..." Janie bounces to a sitting position and throws her pencil gently into my lap. "It's no big deal. About the extra year of school. You know that, right? No one cares!"

I toss her pencil back and flip my braid over my shoulder. My smile feels like a mask. "Thanks, girl."

"Just turn your volume up to 100 and we'll be good to go!"

I'm saved from having to respond to the inaccuracies of that statement by Janie herself—her gaze flicks abruptly over to my desk, and before I can spin to see what she's looking at, she's reached over and scooped my phone into her hand.

"Someone's boyfriend is calling," she laughs, picking up the call and turning the phone to face herself, scooting away from me on the bed. "Hello?" She's laughing, eyes crinkled at the corners, but my stomach drops.

Cam and I usually schedule our video-calls. He must be upset if he's calling now, with no warning. Did he forget Janie and I were studying today? Or is he desperate enough not to care?

"She's here." Janie's still laughing. "But I need to hear the password before I hand you over."

I hold my hand out for my phone, but she pulls away, listening. After a second, she claps a hand over her mouth, eyes wide.

"Oh my gosh!"

"What?" I reach over and tug the phone out of her grasp, flipping it around so I can see Cam's face.

"... too cute!" says Janie in the background, but I'm looking at my boyfriend, whose smile only looks slightly forced.

"Janie's here—obviously," I say, but when he tries to say something back, I can't quite make it out. "Can I call you later?"

He nods and flashes me a thumbs-up and a quick smile.

Okay? I mouth to him, raising my eyebrows to emphasize the question.

He nods, bringing the back of one hand to rest on the palm of the other. GOOD.

"Okay, good," I say out loud. "Talk to you later."

He waves, then ends the call.

"So." Janie leans in, forcing herself into my frame of vision while I'm still staring down at the now-blank screen of my phone. "He's so cute, Skylar! How come you never talk about him? I wasn't even sure the two of you were still together!"

"We're definitely together." I think longingly of our Christmas-break visit to my aunt's in Golden Sound, and how Cam took a few days off school to stay with us during my March break. My parents even let me miss Friday classes to visit him on the weekend last month. "I miss him a lot." I have to find a way to make it to Golden Sound. My parents were fine with a weekend here and there, but can I convince them to let me go away for an entire summer?

I glance down at my phone, firing off a few texts to Cam while Janie prods me for more details.

> *Can you give me more details? Is Ana really leaving? Why is the library closing? Are you okay? What will we do?????*

"Come on, Skylar." Janie knocks the back of my phone with her knuckles. "Why do I feel like you never tell me anything anymore?"

I meet her gaze. My phone lights up with a text, but I force myself not to break eye contact with her. How do I answer that question?

"Never mind," she says, after the pause is just a beat too long. "I guess you're entitled to be mysterious, if you want to."

It's another opening. I could still tell her now—we could have a girl talk gossip session, just like we used to. But where would I even start?

Janie glances back down at her phone, flopping onto her back on my bed. "Hey, Skylar." She holds her phone out to me. "Check this out." It's one of Daria's Instagram posts of her sitting by her backyard pool. "Grad party next week…" says Janie, grinning. "Come on. Say you'll come?"

If I'm here, it might be fun. "Okay." I glance over at Janie, but she's giggling at something on her phone. When I glance over her shoulder, she's watching Instagram stories, not even on Daria's profile anymore.

I should feel disappointed, or lonely, or even a little bit left out. But instead, my chest loosens as I open my own phone and go into my messaging app.

Cam's reply to me is short: *Relax, Sky. I'll call you in half an hour?*

Janie's mom will have picked her up by then, but I don't want to wait.

Is it her daughter? Eva?

Talk soon. I wish there was at least an emoji to follow his response.

"Hey." Janie nudges my knee with her toes. "My mom's going to be here in five."

"I'll help you pack up." Together, we dump stray pencils into their cases, close loose-leaf papers back up into their binders, and toss the remainder of Janie's never-ending stash of study candy back into her backpack. I slip my phone into my pocket and walk Janie downstairs, through the quiet house, and out onto the porch, where we sit on the steps side-by-side, just like we've done since we were kids.

She scrolls through Instagram; I re-read Cam's messages from today and try to figure out what the heck is going on.

When at last her mom's van rolls up, I have to force myself to stand and wave until they're out of sight when all I want to do is get Cam on the video screen across from me, pronto. I punch the video call button before I'm even inside.

At last, his camera turns on, and his grin meets me on-screen. I can't help smiling back.

"Let me get up to my room." I put my mouth close to the speaker, even though I know he can probably hear me just fine. "One sec."

In a quiet room with the sound on my phone turned up all the way, I can usually manage to hear about half of what Cam is saying. If the internet connection is good.

"I have questions." I slam through the front door and lock it behind me—Dad's rule when any of us is home alone. "About Ana. And the library. And everything. And why didn't you respond to any of my texts?" I glance around the kitchen—still empty, Dad must be picking the kids up from school—and flop down at the island counter. "Okay. Empty house. Sound turning on … now." I pin down the volume button and watch the bars increase.

Cam says something, garbled and faint. Tinny. Broken.

"One sec." I train my eyes on his face, ready to watch his lips. "What?"

"I miss you," he says, slow and clear. He's probably yelling. I kind of love him for it.

"Me too." I blow him a kiss. "Now, please, tell me what's going on?"

He opens his mouth to reply.

"No, wait." I hold up a hand. "First, how could you drop that on me over text? And what's with the radio silence after?"

Cam's crooked grin isn't as wide as usual. ALL-DONE? He signs with one hand, eyebrows raised.

I nod.

"… … at the library. I forgot … … my phone." He shrugs, one shoulder hiked exaggeratedly up so I'll be sure not to miss the gesture. "I didn't mean … … you waiting."

"It's okay." I rest my chin in my hands, propping my phone up against the flowerpot by the sink. "So tell me about Ana."

"It's good news," says Cam, and then launches into some sort of story about Ana, her daughter Eva, and a moving truck. I lean as close to the camera as I dare, trying to read his lips and piece together all the different parts of the story. Even with half the conversation missing, I fit here. We understand each other. Five minutes with Cam relaxes me in a way a whole afternoon with my childhood best friend just can't anymore.

"Wait." I cut him off mid-sentence. "Ana's really moving?"

He nods.

"Because of Eva? Or something?"

"She's moving closer to her family." Cam leans toward the phone, and this sentence emerges in a burst of clarity. "But ... ... librarian to replace her."

"Can't you do it?" Cam and I both worked as assistant librarians last summer—he knows how to do it. Plus, he knows the people. And in a small town like Golden Sound, that counts for a lot.

He shakes his head. "They only want me there to pack books. So it's tidy and ready to close."

"Is that it? It's all been decided already?"

Cam rubs his eyes with the tips of his fingers before replying. "Feels that way."

"But it's so well-used!"

He's already nodding along with me. I KNOW.

"Shouldn't the people get a say?"

He shrugs, unbuckling his watch and then fastening it again. And again. "... not."

"Ridiculous." I can't believe they would do this! Not to us. Not to Golden Sound.

"Can you come?" He leans in close to the camera. "Help ... figure it out?"

"Of course."

His face relaxes into a smile—just as wide as I remember. I grin back.

"Is that the only reason you want me to come?" If he was sitting across from me, I'd poke him. Gently. But I have to content myself with verbal jabs instead.

His eyebrows jump up. "Maybe. Maybe not. ... ... show up and find out."

"Meanie."

"I'm teasing, Sky."

There's a flicker of movement by the front door, and I can't help glancing up—away from whatever Cam is saying—to find Sara's face plastered to the narrow window beside the door, peering in at me as Dad fiddles with the lock. By the time I glance back down at the phone, the twins have entered and the sound level in the room has crept up at least triple. I can see Cam's lips moving, but his voice just meshes with the wall of background noise assaulting my hearing aids.

"I can't hear you anymore." I turn the camera to face the twins, who crowd forward. Sara's head almost reaches my shoulder, and when she waves enthusiastically at the camera, she nearly smacks me in the face. "Okay, guys. Clear out. Leave Cam alone."

Sara calls some sort of greeting into the phone and then crosses the kitchen to tug open the fridge. I turn my gaze back to the phone to find a more texts waiting for me.

When you come, I want to take you somewhere special.
On a real date. Not just hanging out at the house together

"You know I like hanging out with you anywhere, right?" But my heart does a little double-beat inside my chest. Spending Christmas and spring break together isn't enough. I miss him like crazy. "Let me go upstairs so we can finish talking."

He shakes his head, points to the text box. *I have to go. Let me know what your parents say?*

I nod. "I'm coming. I'll convince them."

He grins. *That's my girl.*

I'm beaming at him when he disconnects the call, and when Dad waves at me from across the kitchen, laptop balanced precariously on top of the groceries he's supposed to be unloading, I simply re-direct the smile to him.

He spreads his hands wide, palms up.

"Cam." I gesture at the phone, and he nods understandingly. "Hey, Dad?"

He waits, nudging his glasses up to his forehead so he can study me in greater detail.

"Can I drive up to visit Cam after exams?"

He winces. My smile freezes.

"... ... ask your mom."

• ● •

When I pose the question to Mom after work, she sets down her purse, listens patiently as I outline the whole situation, and then puts a hand on my arm. "I'll need to talk to your dad about this one."

"He told me to talk to you!"

"I'm sorry, Skylar." Mom rummages through her purse, passes Sara a bobby pin, licks her thumb and wipes a smear off Aiden's cheek, and then looks back at me. "It's a long trip, and you and Mike share a car ... you've never driven that far alone ..."

"I need to go." I grab her arm so she has to look me in the eyes. "Mom. It's really important."

She meets my gaze, eyebrows pinched just slightly. "Skylar ..."

Mike passes us on his way out the door, guitar case slung over his back. "What's going on?" He leans in over my shoulder, so his words ring clearly through my hearing aids.

"I need to go to Golden Sound." I clench my fists behind my back. "The library is closing, Cam's stressed out—it's really important."

Mike glances over at Mom.

"Your dad and I will discuss it." This is said with finality and a firm nod before she turns to tug the groceries out from under Dad's laptop, half-melted ice cream leaving condensation puddled on the dining room table.

Mike shrugs. "Good luck, Sky." And then he's gone, too, the door swinging shut behind him.

The hour before dinner crawls by. With no homework to do, I trail after Aiden and Sara, allowing them to rope me into playing a round of UNO until Dad comes in with their backpacks and reminds them that even though I'm done with my classes, they still have homework. Then he fixes me with the same look and asks about exams.

I beeline for my room.

When Mom texts an hour later, calling me down for dinner, everyone is already around the table. Except my older brother.

"Where's Mike?" I accept the tray of taco shells half-flung across the table by Sara and slide two onto my plate before handing them off to Dad.

Mom reaches for the salsa, turning her face toward me even though she's looking in the other direction. "Teaching guitar lessons again tonight. He's trying to get as many hours in as possible before that internship starts."

Dad scoops sour cream onto his taco. "I'm really proud of him."

Mom nods. "He's really got himself back on track."

She doesn't say the words *after last summer*, but I know we're all thinking it.

I take a bite of my taco and instantly regret it. Mouth full, I force out the words. "What's his internship, again?" For all intents and purposes, I'm ignored, although it's difficult to say if that's because no one hears me or they're just more focused on Sara and the entire glass of milk she tips into her lap while reaching for the chicken. I wait for a good moment to ask them about my own traveling plans this summer, but a good moment never presents itself.

After dinner, I can't catch either one of them before they vanish into Dad's office, which is mostly just used as storage. I stand outside the door, forehead pressed to the frame, and when Aiden walks by, I grab his arm.

"What are they saying?"

He leans in, presses his ear to the door. His forehead wrinkles. "They're talking about you."

"But what are they *saying*?"

He shrugs. "Can I go now?"

I let go of his wrist and press my forehead against the door, wishing I could hear anything beyond the faint roaring of air in my hearing aids.

Minutes pass.

When someone puts a hand on my arm, I shrug them off, assuming it's Aiden or Sara. "Not now. I'm waiting for Mom and Dad to finish talking about me and come up with some answers."

The pressure increases, and when I turn to scold whichever twin is cutting off my circulation, I find Mike looking back at me instead. He places a finger to his lips, leans his ear against the door, and closes his eyes.

I wait.

Then, without warning, he scrambles back, motioning for me to do the same. I have barely enough time to step back from the doorway when it opens, and my parents step into the hallway.

Mom flicks a suspicious glance between us.

"How was the meeting?" I hold my hands behind my back.

Dad sighs, adjusting his glasses. "Skylar, your mom and I have had a chance to talk, and we've decided that you can spend a weekend or two in Golden Sound this summer, but it's not really reasonable for you to go away for the whole summer."

"But I—"

Mom chimes in, ending my protest before it can really begin. "It's a long time to be away, Skylar. You and Mike share a car, and he's going to need it, too, to drive to his internship."

"Sorry, Sky," mutters Mike into my left ear, exiting the hallway in a hurry. I'm on my own.

"Is that it? Just the car?"

My parents glance at each other. "It's a long time to be away

from your family," adds Mom. "And with your aunt traveling so…
spontaneously…"

That's one word for it.

"We couldn't count on having her there to keep an eye on you."

"I'm not twelve years old. I'll be with Cam! It'll be fine!"

"Why doesn't Cam come here for a little bit?" Dad suggests,
cleaning his eyeglasses on his shirt.

How have they missed the entire point? "But the library is
closing! He can't leave Golden Sound now!"

Mom pulls me in for a hug. "Sometimes this happens with
small towns, sweetie. Things just close."

"I need to go there so I can help him fix this." I know before
the words have left my mouth that it's not going to work. I might
as well be speaking to a wall.

"We can talk about it again tomorrow," says Mom, but I know
I'm not going to change her mind.

How in the world am I going to get to Golden Sound?

Chapter TWO

Mike

First and second term combined average: 61.4%

I SCAN THE WORDS AT THE BOTTOM OF MY TRANSCRIPT OVER AND OVER again, hoping I've just read the numbers wrong. Is there a chance it says sixty-nine instead of sixty-one? Could I email the academic counsellor and ask them to round up?

I swipe at the screen with my finger, cleaning off specks of invisible dirt. Nothing. Sixty-one it is. I don't need to look at the course breakdown to know where my failures are. For a wanna-be business major, seeing a 49 next to my Intro to Business course and a 52 next to Marketing Basics doesn't feel good. I could email my guidance counsellor, but I already know what she'd say.

> *Unfortunately, you'll need to retake both of those courses before applying to the program of your choice in second year. And unfortunately, summer internships are only offered to students with a first-year average above 70%. Would you like to explore some options for retaking those two courses this summer?*

Unfortunately, I want to write back, *I really hated first year. And I have no idea what to do next.*

I refresh the page and squint at the screen one more time, nose practically pressed to the laptop. I can see every pixel of every number, and there's no doubt about it: all my plans for the summer—and maybe the fall, too—are over.

So, what now?

Mom's voice floats up the hall. She's talking on the phone, maybe to Dad. "I'll have to get him to do some shopping," she says, laughing. "He'll need dress pants and more than one button-down, that's for sure."

I prop my forehead in my hands and listen to her conversation as she pads by my door.

"I'll talk to him about it tonight. Yes, I know. It's all happening so fast … I think he's really excited …" she trails off, listening, and by the time she speaks again, she's too far away to hear clearly.

I have to tell her. I imagine the look on her face when she sees my grade. The concern. The fear that I'll spiral again. The instant problem-solving, the phone calls to the school (no, thank you VERY much). Mom going full bear-mode.

I wish I could just hop in the car and drive until my failure felt like a small thing and even my parents' concern couldn't reach me.

Pounding feet run up the stairs and down the hall, and approximately four seconds later, Skylar explodes into my room. "Have you seen my charger?"

I spin around slowly in my desk chair. "Hi, Skylar. Sure, you can come into my room. What do you want?"

She ignores me. "My charger, Mike!" She waves her phone in my face like that's supposed to tell me something. "My phone died halfway through a conversation with Cam."

I shake my head. "Try—"

But she's already gone, slamming the door shut behind her.

"You're welcome," I say to the back of my closed door. I'll have to tell Skylar, too, and then she'll feel like she has to worry about me, as well as Cam and their precious library.

I turn back to my computer, pulling up my university's web

page and scrolling aimlessly through the program options. Nothing looks interesting. All I can see is that dang 61% floating in front of my eyes.

Next, I pull up an online job site. Maybe I could take a year off, make some money to go towards my student debt, and take some time to figure out what degree I actually want to take. I search aimlessly for jobs in all of Ontario, narrowing the location to the Greater Toronto Area, then Ottawa, and then, on a whim, Golden Sound.

The job prospects shrink with the size of the population, but there are still a reasonable number of postings for such a small town. I guess people always need cashiers, dishwashers, and camp counsellors, no matter where you live.

It would be nice to get away from the GTA. And my parents' disappointment. The idea picks up steam in my head. Why couldn't I do it? Just take off across the province, making Skylar's summer in the process. Text my parents the news about school after I figure out a solution. By the time they even realize there was a problem, it will be solved.

The town itself is the only thing that stops me from calling Skylar straight back into my room. After all, can I really find a fresh start in a town where so much went wrong last summer? Even though Eric feels like a distant memory, what about the rest of it? The drinking, the accident…Alex. What if people remember? What if *she* remembers?

But maybe she won't. It's kid stuff, right? A little smoking. A little stealing. It's not like I fired her myself. I was just there when it happened. But no one would think I had anything to do with it. Not now.

It might not be that simple. But I'll deal with that possibility later.

"Skylar!" I open my door and call for her before realizing she can't hear me.

"She's downstairs," yells Sara from her bedroom across the hall.

"Thanks."

I jog down the stairs and find Skylar in the kitchen with Mom, the two of them eating milk chocolate chips straight out of the bag.

"Mike," says Mom, setting down the chocolate, "I wanted to talk to you about—"

"Bad news," I interrupt, tapping a drumbeat out on the counter in front of them. "My internship has been cancelled."

Her face slackens in surprise. It's a white lie, maybe, but it will buy me time to figure out how to tell them really, it's my own fault I didn't get it. "Oh, hon—"

"It's okay though."

Skylar knocks back another handful of chocolate chips and squints at me, furrowing her eyebrows like she's trying to figure out if I'm okay.

"I was thinking, now that I'm free for the summer, I could go with Skylar to Golden Sound."

Her mouth drops open, both hands flying to cover her face.

Mom steps back, like she needs to get some distance between herself and this conversation. "Mike, that's very—"

"Do you mean it?" Skylar shrieks, leaping across the counter to tackle me. I barely manage to stay upright, thumping her on the back until she releases me, coughing. "Mike, really?"

I jam my hands in my pockets and shrug. "It would give me something to do. I can look for a job in town."

Mom tilts her head to one side. "You'd stay with Skylar?"

"Sure."

She stares past me, out the window. "You could visit Aunt Kay, too. After she was sick on that trip to Mexico, I know she's been paying someone to do her lawn, but if you're going to be around..."

I nod. It's a small price to pay.

"Your dad's worried about her," Mom offers, finally making eye contact with me again. "It would mean a lot to him if you could check up on her."

"No problem." This is a lot easier than I expected.

"When can we go?" Skylar bounces on the very tips of her toes. "My last exam is tomorrow morning! Can we leave tomorrow?"

Mom and I say "no" at the same time.

"Just a minute." Mom turns to me. "Mike, are you sure there's no way around this? Have you talked to your guidance counsellor? Can I see the emails?"

"No!"

She and Skylar both stare at me.

"It's okay." Dial it back, Mike. "I'm sure, Mom. I've read them. It's for sure cancelled."

"I'm sorry, Mike." She half looks like she wants to hug me, so I step back like I'm going to walk out of the kitchen.

"So we *can* go tomorrow, then?" Skylar slides the question into the conversation, hoping for an easy yes. I shake my head at her. With Mom, there's no way.

"You need to pack," says Mom, ticking items off her fingers. "And Mike needs to call Aunt Kay, you need to make sure it's okay with Cam's parents for the two of you to stay for longer than a weekend—they have to be *really* okay with it, Skylar, otherwise you can stay with your aunt."

"She lives on the opposite side of town from Cam!" Skylar looks horrified. "I'd only see him, like, twice a week!"

"Well, these are the details you need to figure out before you can leave." Mom reaches for the chocolate again. I back slowly away and jog up the stairs, content to let them figure out the details.

For now, my secret is safe.

• ● •

Mom and Skylar end up compromising on a departure date a week after Skylar's final exam. On the night before we leave, the twins thump down the hall, bickering through my half-open door.

"Mike?"

When I turn, Aiden's hanging on the door frame, leaning into the room.

"What's up?" I hang the headphones around my neck, spinning in my desk chair to look at him.

"Dad says to change the oil in the car before you go." Downstairs, Sara screams his name.

"Okay, I'll do it in the morning." He's grown, like, six inches this year. How much will he grow while we're gone?

He hesitates.

"Is there something else?"

"You guys are coming back, right?" He can't look at me when he says it, like we both know he's really saying *I'm going to miss you* without using those exact words.

"Definitely." I cross the room and mess with his hair, fisting my hands so I can mock-punch him in the upper arm. "Why? Wanna come?"

He leaps back into the hallway, holding his scrawny arms up in the defensive position I taught him.

"AIIIDEN!" Sara shrieks his name from the bottom of the stairs.

"Later, man." I catch one flailing fist and fend off another wild punch. He's stronger than he looks. He flashes me a gap-toothed grin and pounds down the stairs. Guess I solved that problem.

If only I could solve my school issues so easily. I'm going to tell Skylar the truth about the internship—and my failed first year—in the car on the way to Golden Sound. Maybe she can help me figure out a way to tell our parents.

Or, I realize after I've flicked the lights off and crawled into bed hours later, when the twins are asleep and silence reigns, maybe she'll be even more worried than they are. Maybe she'll text Mom and then I'll have everyone on my case, my entire family in Fix-It-For-Mike mode. The thought keeps me awake for hours.

• ● •

By the time we're finally on the road the next day, telling Skylar doesn't feel like such a good idea anymore. I don't notice I've got a death-grip on the steering wheel until she asks who I'm trying to choke. She says it with a laugh, turning to look out the window, but I'm glad for the moment of privacy so I can smooth the reaction out of my features. I thought telling her the truth would be easier than this, but…nope. I failed her in so many ways last summer. I don't know how to admit that I've done it again. I don't want to be that guy anymore.

"I can't believe Mom and Dad let us do this." She's still staring out the window, chin in hand. "I mean, I'm glad they did. You would not *believe* the crap Cam is putting up with in Golden Sound." She turns to look at me, face red. "I mean, he was telling me about this board that they apparently have, like you know, with board members and stuff?"

I nod.

"Anyway, the board makes decisions about publicly-funded programs, but get this: they're not made up of town members, they're mostly bigshots from the overall municipality."

When she says *municipality*, she makes a sweeping motion so large she almost smacks me in the head.

"Anyway, they've just arbitrarily *decided*"—insert dramatic air quotes—"to put in a YMCA, which is actually kind of a good idea, but they want to tear down the old library and put a bigger building in when there's a perfectly good *empty* site just one street over."

At this point, she has to pause for a breath. I'm thinking of jumping in and just dropping my news on her, but before I can say anything, she keeps right on going.

"They want to distribute all the books to the larger, city libraries, and move to an online library service only. So people can order books in and pick them up, but there won't actually be a physical library to browse. No staff. No programs. Just some guy in a truck doing book drop-offs in a small town every Monday." She sounds like she's picking up steam again. "What if you need a book on Wednesday? You just have to wait!"

I have never heard Skylar talk this much about books, ever. "I mean, sure, it sounds sucky, but are you sure you and Cam will be able to change anything? If a board has already made all these decisions?"

"If we can get enough people involved, yes." She's so determined. "We have to try."

I nod along. What else is there to say? Skylar is in full fix-it mode. I'm just glad she's not trying to fix *me*.

"Anyway." She huffs out a huge sigh. "I'm glad they're letting us do this." She's looking out the passenger window, so I don't have to reply right away. "The way Dad looked last week, I thought for sure it was over." She turns her head to look at me.

"You're lucky I didn't get that internship." The joke hurts.

"I'm lucky to have you." She glances out the window again, so I know she's not looking for compliments. I flick my eyes over at her and all I can see is the thin band of plastic behind her ear. Is she lucky to have me? I don't know how true that is.

Skylar's phone buzzes in the cupholder between us.

"Sky." I flip the phone into her lap, and she accepts the call, putting the phone on speaker.

"Hello? Cam?"

His voice echoes through the speaker, crackly and faint. There's no way she'll be able to hear a word.

"Skylar?"

She presses the phone, still on speaker, to the hearing aid behind her ear. "Mike's here, too."

"Hey, man." Cam clears his throat.

"Hey." I flip the fans off altogether. It doesn't really help. "What's up?"

"I've got some bad news."

Skylar's squinting across the dashboard like bringing the horizon into focus will make Cam's words clearer.

"He said there's bad news." I raise my voice, signal, and pull over onto the gravel shoulder. When I flip the key in the ignition, the engine noise dies, but the crease between Skylar's eyebrows remains when Cam speaks again. She still can't hear him.

"What is it, Cam? Can you speak up?" Her knuckles are white on the phone.

He sighs.

Her expression doesn't change.

"They've made a final decision. They're closing the library, effective immediately. Demolition will begin in September so they can build the new building in the new year."

I repeat this, staring past her shoulder so I don't have to see her face drop at the news.

"No!" She pulls the phone away from her ear, shakes it slightly, and replaces it. "They can't! Tell them they can't do it! There's enough interest—people love the library! It's a community hub! They have to keep it open for tourist season, then they'll see! The town *needs* this."

Cam's voice cuts through the chatter, but Skylar's talking over him. The two of them talking at full volume in the passenger seat rings in my ears.

I grab Skylar's arm. "One sec. He's talking."

She yanks away from me, but snaps her mouth shut. "Cam?"

His voice sounds strained. "I tried."

I repeat this to Skylar.

"There has to be something we can do." She fiddles with the seat belt buckle, eyebrows furrowed deeply.

Cam is silent on the other end of the line, so I nod at her to keep going.

"What does Ana think?"

"She's already gone."

I repeat this, too.

"Mike and I will be there soon." She sits up a little straighter, mouth firming at the corners. This is Skylar ready for action. Whoever's in charge of the library doesn't stand a chance. "Cam, we can get the community involved in this. We can put up posters. We can make enough noise that they *have* to listen to us."

"I don't know, Sky." He sounds tired.

When I repeat his words, she bites the corner of her lip. "Can we talk about it when I get there? Mike will help, too!" She mouths the word *please* at me. I flash her a thumbs-up. "He can run the social media platforms for us. He's working on a business degree, and now that his internship is cancelled, he has more free time." She raises her eyebrows at me, waiting.

There's no way. I flinch, but she takes it for a nod.

"He said yes! He'll do it!"

No. No way. *Speak up, Mike. Fix it now.* I open my mouth to say something, but then Cam clears his throat. "Okay."

I clear my own throat. Skylar's beaming. Maybe I can do this for them. Maybe if I can succeed at this, it will soften the blow about school. Make it seem like it was the right thing, to end on a high note and just move on. "He said yes."

"Yes!" She pumps a fist in the passenger side. "Awesome! Don't worry, Cam." She's grinning, flipping her hair over her shoulder with one hand. "We're going to do this. We can save the library."

It's so simple to her, so easy for her to believe that things will work out the way they're supposed to. But she didn't hear the pause. The sigh. The exhaustion in Cam's voice. I wonder what else is going on. What parts of the story he hasn't told her yet. How she'll react if it all doesn't go according to plan.

"Okay," she says, her lips next to the speaker. "I'll text you when we're getting close. Bye." After a long pause, she ends the call, slipping the phone back into the console between us. "We're going to do this."

I can't tell if she's trying to convince me or herself.

"Good for you." I turn the car back on and pull out onto the road. I won't tell her about the way Cam sounded on the phone. She can figure that out for herself.

"Thanks for helping."

Should I tell her the truth about the internship now?

"It won't take long—"

I tune her out as she starts to talk about plans, schedules, what I can do on the days when I'm not working.

"Why *did* you agree to come?"

Here it is. Time to tell her. But I just can't find the words.

"Mike?"

"I wanted to get out of the house for a bit." I clench the steering wheel. I can't do it. Can't burst her bubble like this. Shoot. How did I end up here? "I don't know, Skylar. Don't you get tired of being home all the time?"

She nods, pulling her hair back over her shoulder and twisting it together into some kind of braid. "I get that." We drive in silence for a minute or two. "I'm glad."

I don't ask what she's so happy about, but I can feel her looking at me and I'm pretty sure she's going to tell me anyway.

"I missed you this year." She flicks my shoulder with the tip of her finger. "Hello? Are you listening?"

"Trying to drive." I almost wince as I say it, hoping she won't pick up on my short tone. Maybe this is all I'm destined to be. The screw-up older brother. I keep finding myself here. Over and over again.

"I was worried about you. After last year. And then when you moved away for school."

"Well, you don't need to worry anymore." I force a smile, make a turn onto a gravel road. The sun is in my eyes.

"I'm glad you're back." She grins. "Mostly because it means the summer of car-sharing has begun, but—"

"Whatever." I reach to pinch her shoulder, but she ducks out of reach.

Skylar falls asleep in the passenger seat a few minutes later, and

I'm left alone with the radio and the long, empty roads, lulled into a strange feeling of nonexistence—we're neither here nor there, neither departing nor arriving. In transit. In uncharted, unfamiliar territory where nobody knows who we are. Or what we've done.

The first landmark that slides by is the place where I crashed the car. It looks so exactly like every other country road, every other ditch, that I almost don't notice. It's the bend in the road that snags my memory, the feeling of my hands on the wheel and the steady, urgent pressure of the brake pedal underneath my feet. The yellow arrows and the sign marked Corner 60kph.

Now, like then, I take the turn too fast. But this time, I'm not drunk. And Eric isn't beside me, hauling on my arm. Skylar doesn't even wake up, just turns her head to the side as I slow the car down and finish the turn, eyes off the ditch where I rolled the car the last time I was here.

I drive a little slower on the other roads into town, ignoring the GPS. I used to drive this route a lot—past the McDonald's on the outskirts of town and straight into the heart of Golden Sound. We'd take this way home from work, often running the broken red light at the center of town.

Before I've realized what I'm doing, I've missed the turn to Aunt Kay's. I'm cruising straight down Main Street, headed for Eric's house on the other side of town.

Skylar wakes up halfway through my three-point turn. "What's going on?"

"Missed my turn." I almost yell the words, so she'll hear me without me having to look right at her.

"Cam's is that way," she says, pointing toward Eric's house. "He lives way out in the country, remember?"

I forgot we were staying with him instead of in Aunt Kay's house. I'll check on her tomorrow instead.

I reverse my way out of my turn and continue down Main Street, reminding myself to loosen my hands on the wheel. *How* am I going to tell my sister the truth? Maybe I can text her tomorrow. Maybe it doesn't have to be face-to-face.

"Eric lives around here, doesn't he?" Skylar cranes her neck, peering out the window as we pass his street.

"Yeah." I'm surprised she remembers. She's only been there once. I swear I smell beer when I drive by his street.

"Mike?"

She didn't hear me. "Yes, he does." I say the words again, louder. She nods. "I wonder what he's up to this summer."

I don't know why she's talking about this—if she's testing me to see how I'll react, or if she's bored and trying to make conversation. I shrug one shoulder. "Who knows? I don't care." Beside me, I see her satisfied nod, shoulders relaxing as she rests her feet on the glove compartment. She's still worried about me. Again. I wish I could remember a time when I wasn't the concern of the family—the one everyone watched and whispered about.

"Look!" She leans forward, unbuckling her seat belt. "There's the house number! This is it!"

I grab her arm before she can fling the door open and leap out, the car still rocketing forward at full speed. "I see it. Chill out." The little green sign at the end of the country driveway reads 4420. Someone is standing on the porch.

"Cam!" shrieks my sister, and I slam the brakes so she can open the car door and sprint the last hundred meters toward him.

I ease the car up the driveway and put it in park as she flings herself into his arms. I'm a coward. And I've just made it even harder for myself to tell her the truth.

Chapter
THREE

Skylar

I DON'T REALIZE I'VE FORGOTTEN SHOES UNTIL I FEEL THE PEBBLE DIGGING into my heel as I fling my arms around Cam, burying my face in his neck. His shoulders are firm beneath my tight grip, and I can feel him laughing as he squeezes me, one hand finding the back of my neck. We've hugged before, but not in months, not since March break. Ages ago. For one awkward moment, it feels strange, like I've hugged some random guy on the bus, and then I think furiously to myself, *but this is Cam*, and everything snaps back into place again. We're good.

He taps his fingers on my shoulder after a minute, tugging me back a few inches so I can see his face. "I missed you."

"I can't believe I'm really here." The more I look at him, the more the year between us—between last summer and now—seems to shrink. All the video calls and visits over the holidays feel realer than all the time we spent apart, combined.

Cam's gaze flicks above and behind me, toward Mike. When I turn, he's lifting suitcases out of the back of the van, a wry smile on his face.

"I said, I can." He lifts his chin, like changing the angle of his head will make it easier to hear him. "I drove the whole ... ... you slept."

I turn my back on the car again, unable to keep the smile off my face. "I offered to drive! You just didn't want to switch."

Cam's smile creases the skin under his eyes, and he reaches out a hand for me, shadows in the hollows beneath every bone as they curve beneath his skin. He's always been slim—athletic—but was he this skinny when I saw him in March? I can't remember.

"Did you ace the final or what?" Cam reaches for a high-five, and I smack his palm.

"You know I did. The Bradys crushed it this year at school. Right, Mike?" I turn to bring him in on the high-five, too, only he's not behind me. He's back at the car, head ducked down, fiddling with a suitcase.

He raises a hand in acknowledgement, but I'm still left hanging.

"Anyway." I hope I'm not blushing when I turn back to Cam.

"Want to come inside?" Cam reaches for one of the suitcases Mike is lugging towards us. "It's kind of crazy in there right now ... kids have friends over and they've .... backpacks in the entryway ..."

I swing a bag over my arm next to my purse and follow him to the door. Cam pulls it open and holds it for me, but when I walk through and into the front hall (stepping over a discarded backpack...or four) he doesn't follow me. Instead, he's saying something to Mike, who lugs the last suitcase one-handed up the driveway, his head ducked down. What's wrong with him? He was fine in the car.

"Mike!" By the way their heads snap around, I guess I've put too much frustration into my tone. "Sorry." I intentionally try to relax the muscles in my throat, breathe calmly, relax my shoulders. "I just wanted..." What did I want? "...you to hurry up."

Mike shrugs. "Sorry, Your Highness." He hefts the suitcase

over the threshold. "I ... ... a minute." The front door falls shut behind him, enclosing us in the front room.

We hover in the front entrance for only a moment longer. Just as Cam is about to say something, an entire flock of pre-teens floods the room, followed by Cam's parents.

"Skylar, it's so good to see you!" Cam's mom folds me in a hug while his dad shakes Mike's hand. I realize a second too late that Mike hasn't met Cam's parents before. I should be introducing them. Oops.

"This is my brother, Mike." When Cam's mom steps back from the hug, I wave one hand in Mike's general direction, dropping my purse next to his suitcase. "He worked at the McDonald's in town last summer, but now he's at school for business. He's going to help us with all of our social media promotions for the 'save the library' campaign."

Mike twitches his lips into a smile. Maybe he's just nervous.

Cam mumbles something to Mike (probably *"We appreciate it, man"* or whatever else guys say to each other when they're trying to be cool).

"Well, that sounds great." Cam's dad places his hands on his lap, grinning around the room at all of us. Across the hall, one of Cam's younger sisters sticks her head into the room, waves at me, and then calls something to her mom, who mouths *talk to you later* to me and then exits.

Cam grins again, his fingers fiddling with his watchband before he rips his hand away, like he's trying to break the habit. "Do you want to unpack now?"

Mike's already nodding, but my idea of unpacking is nothing more than unzipping my suitcase.

"No, it's—"

Mike tugs the bag out of my hand and hoists it and the other one he's carrying into the air. "You guys go. Have fun."

Oops. I shouldn't ditch Mike right away. "Actually." I reach to put an arm around Cam's waist, hesitate—after all, Mike is right there—and tap his shoulder, instead. "Let me go put a few things away, okay?"

He looks a little surprised, until he follows my gaze to where Mike is just reaching the top of the stairs. "Is everything okay?"

I jog up the first few steps and then turn. "Yep. Really."

He picks up my purse, which I don't remember setting down. "I believe you." But he wiggles his eyebrows when he says it, so I can't tell if he really does or not.

I reach back to take the purse from him and bound up the stairs, crashing through the first door on the right to find Mike, suitcase unzipped, folded clothes already in stacks by the empty closet.

"You're hanging your shirts up?"

He gives me an eyebrows-lowered glare, and I lift my hands in surrender. "Sorry. Never mind."

"We are going to be here all summer, you know." He carries on unpacking. His clothes are all folded in his suitcase. Classic Mike. I think of my own suitcase, clothes stuffed in whatever rumpled way makes most sense. It's amazing, honestly, that we're even related.

I reach for the zipper that encloses the left half of his suitcase, trying to make it look like I came in here for a reason other than checking up on him.

"So." I lift out a green shirt, shake it out, and slide it onto a hanger. "What are you up to this afternoon?"

Mike turns toward me so I can see his face when he answers. "Skylar. Go have fun. Stop worrying about me." He takes the hanger from me, pulls the shirt off it, and puts it back on the other way.

Am I that transparent? I can feel myself blushing. "It's just… you were going to spend all summer at your internship. And now you're here. And I don't want you to be…I don't know. Lonely."

He closes his eyes like he's in pain. Or tired. Or both? "It's fine. Really. You're not abandoning me. Go have fun."

I open my mouth to argue.

"I'm going to job-search. I'll be fine." He hangs another shirt and turns to me.

"Okay." I lift out a pair of running shorts and then just shove them back in without re-folding them. Mike must be the exception to the rule. No one folds shorts. Do they?

"Skylar." Mike extracts the shorts I just crumpled, pulls the suitcase gently away from me, and zips it shut. "Go. Please."

"Okay!" I slide off the bed and walk to the door, turning in the doorway to see if he's changed his mind.

Like he expected me to stop, Mike's already looking at me, pointing toward the stairs. But he's smiling.

My suitcase is waiting at the door of the room next to Mike's, so I just open the door and roll it inside. Unpacking done, Skylar-style. I cross the hall and peer into the bedroom across from ours, trying to remember where Cam's room is.

A teenage girl with her hair in braids—not one of Cam's siblings—glances over at me and points down the hall to the left. She says something that I can't hear, and I call a thank you over my shoulder before poking my head in the next door down. Bingo.

Cam is lying on his stomach across the bed, phone in hand. When he sees me, he grins.

I lean against the doorframe. "Want to go for a walk?"

He reaches for a set of car keys on the side table. "Here? Or in town?"

I close my eyes and picture Main Street—the library, the little grocery store, and the rustic café. "Let's go to Milk and Sugar."

Cam grimaces, swinging his feet off the bed.

"What?" I look up at him as he passes me, running his fingers down my arm so my skin tingles.

"I meant to tell you." He glances back at me so I can read his lips as we walk down the hall toward the stairs.

I stare at him. "What happened?"

He sighs—I can see his shoulders heave as he jogs down the

stairs. When we reach the bottom, he turns to face me. "It's the only bad part about living in a small town. Same with the library. Sometimes places just don't get enough people. And then they have to close."

I think of the little café with the big windows, the warm chocolate chip cookie the girl behind the counter gave me for free. I only went once. I always meant to visit again. "It's just…gone?"

He nods. "The girl who ran the shop moved to the city to do another degree. She sold it to an insurance company."

The boring realities of an insurance company—what a waste of windows!—take my breath away. "But that was the only coffee shop."

Mike appears at the top of the stairs. He says something to Cam, thumping down each step so loudly that I can't make out a single word. Before I can ask for a translation, he pulls his keys out of his pocket and slams out the door, jogging down the driveway toward the van.

"Where's he going?" I squint at the car as it reverses down the driveway, spitting up gravel as it turns the corner. Mike drives back toward Golden Sound. Why?

"Didn't say." Cam sits down on the steps, leaning back on his elbows. "Sky, come on."

"What?"

He nudges my shin with his toe. "You're helicopter sistering."

For a moment, I think I've heard him wrong, but when he sees the confusion on my face Cam fingerspells it for me. Twice.

"With good reason, though." I lean against the wall, wishing I could sit next to him but knowing I'd lose the ability to read his face.

"It's been a year."

We both stare at the front door, the screen hanging an inch away from the frame. It bounced after Mike closed it behind him, and now it swings, gently, in the breeze from the porch.

"Anyway," Cam says softly, drumming his fingertips on my

knee. "All is not lost when it comes to the coffee situation in Golden Sound."

"No?"

"Don't laugh." The corners of his mouth betray his desire to do just that. I've missed all the tiny nuances of his face. The lines a video call just can't capture. "But another place did open up."

"Why would I laugh at that?"

He shakes his head. "It was a pre-existing business that bought up the café equipment and set it up just in the doorway of their store. So there's no sit-in area. More like just a walk-up."

He's drawing out the details of this story so slowly, leading up to the punch line. But so far, I don't see anything funny about it.

"So?" I rest my hands on my hips. "Where is this business slash coffee bar?"

"You know what?" Cam looks delighted, rising to his feet and planting a kiss on my cheek before leaning back so I can see his face. "Let's go there. We can take my car."

I try not to look like I'm looking for Mike as I climb into the passenger seat, checking the mirrors to see if our shared car has reappeared at the head of the driveway. Cam's free hand finds mine and squeezes. "Skylar. Stop it."

"I'm not!" I glance over at him. "How did you know?"

He laughs. "You have a 'worrying-about-Mike' face." He squishes up his eyebrows and catches his bottom lip between his teeth in an exaggerated imitation of me.

I smack his shoulder. "Okay, I get it. I swear I won't think about him anymore."

"It's just us." I can't tell if he says *finally* out loud or if I just imagine the word settling comfortably between us.

I've been waiting such a long time for this.

Cam tells me more about Anastasia as we drive: how her sister invited her to come and stay, how a house in their city became Ana's dream home. How she cried when she said good-bye. And then, the way the phone calls came in hot like arrows fired from a taut bowstring, like they'd been looking for an excuse to close the library for a long time.

"Who knows?" Cam signals and pulls into a parking spot on the street right in front of the library. "Maybe they were."

I dart a glance across the street to see if Mike has parked there. Nope. "We won't let them." I focus on Cam's face, the asymmetric tilt of his lips as he watches me. 100%, he knew I was looking for Mike. Oh, well. "We can fight this," I say out loud. "They're just expecting to close the library because no one will resist. But we can show them how much the town needs it."

"Do you ... ..." The rest of Cam's sentence is lost as he climbs out of the driver's seat and shuts the door. I catch up with him somewhere between the headlights and thread my fingers through his.

"Do I what?"

He looks tired. Older than I remember him, like a middle-aged businessman coming home after a long day at the office. Is the library doing this to him?

"Do you think we can beat them? The board?"

I squeeze his hand. "You're not doing this alone anymore. I'm here now, and Mike's going to just absolutely handle the whole social media side of things, so we can focus on the library, and the people, and the town."

He leans his head down, bumping his chin into my shoulder. "That's one thing we don't have to think about, at least."

He's right. Mike is going to be a *huge* help. Yet another reminder of how much things have changed.

"There's a lot of people counting on us," Cam says, swinging our joined hands between us as we cross the street. "I've been fielding questions since Ana announced she was leaving."

"And now we'll field them together."

He sucks in a breath. "Where do we even start?"

"Hey." I pull him to a stop on the sidewalk. "We'll figure it out. I promise." I've never seen Cam like this before.

I tear myself away from my thoughts and glance up at the sign now dangling above our heads. *Storyteller's* is spelled out in swirly cursive font, and then beside it, *Tattoo Parlor.*

"Is this—"

Cam points to the window, where a handmade sign reads *and coffee bar.*

"You've got to be kidding me." I want to laugh, but something in my chest pinches. They got rid of Milk and Sugar for this? And now they want to take my library, too?

"You're not laughing." Cam swings an arm around my shoulders. "Huh? Skylar?" His lips brush the back of my ear, his words loud and clear. Or at least, as close to clear as I'm ever going to get. "I thought you'd think it was funny."

"It is." I glance up again, notice the delicate hand-lettering, the glint of a freshly shined latte machine positioned just inside the window. Someone has taken a lot of care with the leftovers of my favorite café. It hasn't been abandoned or forgotten.

But it isn't anywhere close to being the same.

"… … inside." Cam links arms with me, pulling my head down to rest on his shoulder for just a second while he swings the door open. My phone buzzes in my pocket, but when the smell of chocolate chip cookies hits me, I forget to check the screen. There's a small jar of cookies sitting on the counter, and although the woman behind the counter is different than the one who ran the café, her smile is kind. The creases at her eyes look worn and weary, her knuckles rubbed raw like she's had her hands in hot water all day, but she seems pleased to see us. She exchanges pleasantries with Cam, all of which are folded behind her stiff lips and buried beneath the hissing of the milk steamer. But the chocolate chip cookie is good enough to dull my other senses, the chips still warm and gooey against my tongue.

I don't even notice when my phone stops ringing.

Chapter FOUR

Mike

I HAVE NO IDEA WHERE I'M GOING, BUT I HAVE TO GET OUT OF THAT HOUSE. Only Skylar would be able to raise the hopes of an entire family in the first five minutes of getting there. Only Skylar could find a way to pin it all on me.

The question is...where am I going to go now? If this was last summer, I'd take off in search of Eric, looking to drown my emotions in the better part of a six-pack or the sweet taste of a joint on my breath. But I swore I wouldn't go back to that, so where does that leave me now?

I guess I could check on Aunt Kay.

I slow the car down when I hit the town line, inching my way down Main Street and waiting at least five minutes at that old, broken red light. I forget what Mom said she was sick with—an infection of some kind? It must be more serious than the flu if she's still not back to normal after weeks in Canada. I assume she's not contagious.

When at last the stoplight blinks green, I make a left turn and then a right onto Aunt Kay's street, the water rippling gently in the distance. I remember coming down this street hungover, when the lake was dark and the sun was rising out the back window of the car. I remember the way Eric's backseat reeked of old fries and beer, but when we were all buzzed, not quite drunk yet, it was nice to be a part of something. When the practical side of my brain had gone to sleep and life was a challenge we'd already won…that was a good place to be. On my bad days, I still miss it.

Aunt Kay is sitting on her front porch when I pull the car into the driveway. She meets me at the top of the steps when I get out of the car, pulling me into a bone-crushing hug. I guess she's not *that* sick. But when I pull back, she looks smaller than I remember, and just a little bit pale.

"Oh, Micah!" She's the only one who calls me by my full name. "I didn't know you were coming today!"

"Neither did I." Before I can explain, she's already turning back to the two seats on the front porch, gesturing for me to join her. Her hands shake a little bit, and when she flops down in the seat, she looks winded. "Oh, I haven't quite kicked this bug yet," she says, waving a hand dismissively when she sees me staring. She moves like an old woman, but she's only a few years older than my dad. "I'll be fine. Stop looking at me like that. Come sit down here and tell me about you!"

I sit down on the edge of the other chair. "Are you sure you're okay?" It feels wrong not to ask. Even if I don't know what to do with the answer.

Aunt Kay heaves a sigh and closes her eyes, folding her hands like she's praying for patience. "You and my doctor both. I picked up a little infection while I was traveling, and yes, it's knocked the stuffing out of me in a few different ways, but I am truly on the mend. I'm even taking most of the medications they're prescribing me!"

That should be the bare minimum, but I guess it counts as a victory?

"A few more weeks and I'll have all my strength back. That's what the medical professionals say." She opens her eyes again and folds her arms. "Now, I haven't seen you in such a very long time."

Her eyes soften at the corners, creasing into the same smile wrinkles as Dad. "How are you, Micah?"

"I'm good." I shrug, resting my hands on my knees.

"Are you really?" Aunt Kay leans forward, putting a hand on top of mine. "You look like something's on your mind."

I almost laugh. When, in the last two years, has something *not* been on my mind? "It's just the normal stuff. Growing up. School. You know."

"Ah, yes!" She squeezes my hand and sits back again. "Your mom and I were talking about your internship just the other day. It's such a shame they had to cancel it, but you'll have lots of other chances. In fact, I was talking to a friend of mine who works in accounting, and she said—"

"The internship didn't cancel." I can't listen to one more person trying to help me make connections. There's no way.

Aunt Kay pauses, but she doesn't look surprised. "Oh?"

I suck in a deep breath. "I failed a few courses in first year and wasn't eligible anymore. I can't go into second year without re-taking classes in the summer."

Aunt Kay doesn't say anything.

"I'm here, obviously." I laugh, but it sounds forced even to me. "Not at school. I don't know what I'm going to do in the fall. And I haven't told my parents."

My aunt nods along with every word.

"Or Skylar. Actually—" I run a hand over the back of my head. Man, it feels good to get this out. "Actually, she thinks I'm going to use all of the schooling that I didn't actually learn last year to help them save the library, so I'm kind of—" I suck back the swear word at the last second. "Kind of screwed. To be honest."

"Wow, kid." My aunt leans her head against the back of the chair. "That's a lot, huh?"

I lean my elbows on my knees and stare at my hands. "Yep."

"Is there anything I can do to help?"

"Don't tell my parents."

She raises one eyebrow at me.

"I won't do anything stupid, I promise." I tug my phone out of my pocket and open my job-searching app. As if on cue, Mom texts. I swipe the notification away before I can read more than the preview, which says *I've been thinking about that internship! :-) Have you thought of ...*

"I'm trying to find a job, save some money." I hold the phone to my aunt. "I just want to have something figured out before I tell them."

"So, you are planning to tell them at some point?" She reaches out a finger, swipes through a few of the ads I've saved. Favorites a few more I hadn't decided on yet. Then sits back.

"I will. I just need to find the right moment."

"Well, don't wait too long." She raises her hands when I glance over. "I won't tell them. As long as you keep me updated." She leans in and nudges my arm with her fingertips. "You need at least one adult on your side."

"Thanks, Aunt Kay."

She nods. "So, did you just come here for confession, or did you have something you needed to ask me?"

I stand, running my hands down my pants. "Mom told me to check in on you while we're in town. Something about mowing your lawn?" It is, I now notice, freshly cut, with trimmings sprayed across the driveway.

"If I'd known you were coming, I would have saved it for you." She grins. "You can do it next week, okay?"

"Sounds good." I jangle my keys in my pocket. What's the best way to politely leave a conversation? "Uh, do you need anything else?"

She shakes her head. "I'm fine here. The neighbors said they'd bring over something for dinner tonight. I don't think they appreciated the smoke coming from the windows after last night's failed attempt."

Well, at least that explains where Skylar gets her lack of baking genes from.

"Get out of here." She makes a shooing motion with her hands. "Go find yourself a great job this summer, okay?"

"I'll try." I jog down the steps and slide into the driver's seat. I really need to get those social media accounts up and running. Maybe I'll get a few of them up now, before I look for jobs. I put the car in reverse and back down Aunt Kay's driveway, waving at her once more before turning onto the main road.

I drive through residential neighborhoods, back in the direction of Main Street. I need somewhere with Wi-Fi…and a hefty amount of peace and quiet. When I reach the main strip, I pull to the side of the road and search for free Wi-Fi signals. Bingo. There's one called *Storyteller's*, and it's got four bars. I roll the windows down in the car, turn off the engine, and open Instagram. Using an old image of the library I found online, I mock up a profile and set the privacy settings to public. Then I do the same for Twitter and Facebook. I hesitate over YouTube and TikTok, but if we're not going to shoot video content, there's no point in even creating the accounts. The library already has a website, so I link it to all of the social media accounts and put up a post on each using the hashtag #SaveSmallTownLibraries.

I'm doing it. Now all I've got to do is get some posts up and watch the followers roll in. I shoot Skylar a celebratory text (*social media profiles = up and running*), and when I'm satisfied, I open up my profile on the job search website.

• ● •

I've only made a few searches, sent my resume off to a handful of companies, when someone's shadow looms out my window.

I almost jump out of my skin when I look up and see Eric looming over my open window. His truck is parked in front of my car—how did I not notice him pulling up?—and a blunt rests loosely between his lips.

"Returning to the scene of the crime, huh?" Cigarette smoke wafts over me, the sweet smell of marijuana snapping me back to last summer so fast I feel whiplash throbbing deep in the base of my skull.

"Hey." I lean my elbow on the window. The scene of the crime...which one? I try not to picture the car, careening around the corner after dark, the taste of beer on my tongue. Try not to picture Alex's face, the smell of salty McDonald's fries, the way the money felt curled in my palm. I haven't thought about half that stuff in months. There's a reason my last conversation with Eric ended with me just walking away.

"I thought I saw you in the car." Eric puts a joint to his lips, draws air through it, and puffs it all out his nose. I almost gag. The memories are too strong. "What are you doing back here, man? Did you come to see me?"

His eyes are glassy, red-rimmed, and his smile is loose. He might not even remember this conversation tomorrow. I certainly didn't expect him to remember what we did last summer. He doesn't *look* intimidating, but that's his secret. He's unpredictable. And this is why I left town instead of dealing with him.

"Definitely not." I wish I had a beer. Or three. I never remembered stuff like this when I was drunk.

He laughs long and hard at this, ending with a few gusty coughs.

"I'm gonna go." I twist the key in the ignition, the car humming to life beneath my feet. "See you around."

"Hey, not so fast." Faster than I'd expect from someone as high as he is, Eric flicks his joint through my window. It lands on the passenger seat. "I wanna talk to you."

I grab the joint, stub it out on the car door, and toss it under the wheels. "What the heck, man? What's your problem?" It's scary how easy it is to slide back into the Mike of last summer. When I used to fit in with guys like Eric. He's at least a head shorter than me, but I remember him as being huge. Commanding. Someone you don't want to cross. I wonder if I imagined him bigger last summer, or if he's really shrunk a little bit while I was away at school. His skin doesn't fit him as well as it used to, and he moves like he knows it, like there's a tag scratching him somewhere.

"Your sister?" He says this like it's a question, even though he hasn't asked one.

I wait. With Eric, it's better not to try to guess what he's saying. Sometimes, with very little effort, he can turn your assumptions—or your fears—into reality. Complicated.

"She here too?" He steps back, and I take the opportunity to open my door and stand up, facing him. Being taller than him, looking down slightly to meet his gaze, should make me feel better. But all I can think about are all the ways he could ruin her summer, too.

I don't want Eric anywhere near my sister again.

"Huh? Mike?" He subs the M in my name for a D, chuckles to himself, repeats it a few times under his breath. I'm hoping he'll forget all about Skylar, but when I reach for my keys, step like I'm going to slide into the driver's seat, his gaze narrows, zooms straight in on my face. "You didn't answer my question."

She's going to be all over town. She'll be with Cam. He'll definitely realize she's here. Lying will only tie me to him in a way I'm not eager to step into again. So I tell him the truth.

He laughs. "Bring her along to a party sometime, huh? She'd be a good time."

"I don't think so." I try to keep my tone easy, but it's difficult to get the words out through clenched teeth.

"Aw, relax, man." He slaps me on the shoulder. "I'm just having fun."

"Don't." I work my hands into fists in my pockets. "I'm serious. Don't mess with my sister. And, starting now, you can leave me alone too."

"Come on, Mike." He leans against my car, tapping his fingers on the roof. "I'm just messing. Can't you take a joke?"

When I don't reply, he keeps talking, unbothered.

"Look, man, there's a party at Britt's tonight, and I'm bringing something special."

I don't ask.

"Better than last summer." His eyes are wide, far away, ecstatic. Remembering. "You'll love it. But it'll cost you."

"No." I'm done with him. And I sure don't want whatever it is he's taking. Whatever has him hooked.

Eric's face does that sharpening thing again, like he's zoning into me in a way that cuts through the high. Straight to the kind of point I don't want to make. "What? You don't want to hang out with the boys this summer?"

I stand taller, push my shoulders back a little. I'm not afraid of him anymore. The thought is startling, but it shoots straight through my spine when I realize it's true. "No. I'm done with you and the rest of them. I'm here for Skylar this summer." Here to make a fresh start.

His smile opens so slowly it takes me a minute to realize what I'm looking at. "Are you sure you're ready to handle the…" He fishes for the word. "…consequences of that decision?"

"I'm sure." I open the driver's door, stick the keys in the ignition, and slide into the seat.

Eric leans his forearms on the window, poking his head into the car. "Okay, then. That's up to you."

I put the car in reverse and ease on the gas, just a little, but he doesn't step back. He trips, stumbles, white-knuckled grip on the car door keeping him upright.

He's laughing, scuffing dust up as he steadies himself. "Funny guy, funny guy. I bet you'll laugh real hard when I tell her what really happened last summer."

I don't know how he does it. It's like he can stop being high at a moment's notice, look straight through me, and see exactly what

I'm afraid of. Another secret I'll have to keep from my sister. One I never thought anyone else would remember.

"You can't prove it." It's a weak argument. "I don't care." This one is weaker.

Eric grins. The points of his canines make it look like a snarl. "Oh, I can. I just have to drop a few names, jog a few memories. Mention Alex. Do you remember Alex?"

A long, blonde braid. Tearstains on the front of her uniform. *I need this job*, she'd said. I *swear, I didn't take the money—*

"The police might press charges," Eric continues. "Theft. Alex could sue for…" He slips, the high pushing specific words out of reach. "…something. She could definitely sue you for something."

She probably could, too. Defamation? I try to remember exactly what that means. Can't.

"So let me ask you again." The smile has become a grimace, teeth bared, eyes narrowed. "Are you sure you don't want to hang out this summer." There is no question mark at the end of his sentence.

"What do you want, Eric?" A dangerous question to ask. But right now, it's the only one I've got.

"The stuff I'm on doesn't pay for itself." He leans in. "I'm just asking you to chip in your part. Contribute." He drawls the word out, longer than I thought possible. "Help a buddy out. You know I'd do the same for you."

"Would you?"

"I came through last summer, didn't I?"

Eric is the only reason I didn't end up arrested last summer. But in hindsight, I'm not sure that's something to be thankful for.

"Didn't I? Huh?"

I rest my foot on the gas, just enough to crawl the car back a few inches.

"Hey!" Eric slams both palms against the car, head thrust through the window. I flinch, jam my foot on the gas, and spin the tires as the car jumps back. Eric is thrown to the side and ends up on his hands and knees, shaking his head but otherwise unharmed.

An instinctive apology rises in my throat, but I choke it back. Instead, before he can rise to his feet, I lock the doors and shift into drive, leaving Eric to get to his feet and swing himself back into his truck alone.

I'm only a few blocks away when my phone buzzes, his name lighting up the notifications. I don't have to pick up my phone to read the message, which sears itself across my retinas.

We're not done.

Chapter
FIVE

Skylar

I DON'T REALIZE THAT THE MISSED CALL IS FROM MIKE UNTIL CAM AND I ARE home again, trying to decide where to spend our very first evening together. He's just suggested a movie night, as long as we're okay with the younger teenagers sneaking in to watch with us, when I pull my phone from my pocket and see the notification.

My heart rate instantly spikes.

"Skylar?"

I hear Cam say my name but miss the rest of his sentence, fingers fumbling to find the *return call* button. "It's Mike."

Cam says something else to me that I don't catch, no longer paying attention. Mike's phone rings, and I stare at the screen and wait for him to pick up the call so I can give Cam the phone. He doesn't.

Cam puts a hand on my arm. I redial and force myself to look at him.

"What happened?"

"Mike called me."

Relief flashes across his face. "That's all?"

Mike declines my call again, so I set my phone down on the counter. "Should I call 9-1-1?"

"What?" Cam's eyebrows pucker. "Why?"

I guess he's right. Maybe I'm overreacting. I say this out loud to Cam, and he grins.

"A little bit."

But I can't forget about Mike, even though Cam tries to distract me by putting me in charge of finding a movie while he rummages in the cupboards for snacks.

Please, God. I send up another version of the same prayer I've been repeating all year. *Help Mike. Just…help him.* I'm not sure if it's his cancelled internship or all the memories that must be flooding back after last summer, but something is off with him. For sure.

Right on cue, my brother walks through the door, slipping off his shoes and placing them neatly in the closet.

Cam turns to get my attention, then realizes I'm already looking. Mike, seemingly unaware of the worry he's inspired this afternoon, nods shortly at the two of us and then bounds toward the stairs.

"Mike!"

Cam jumps. In my excitement, I must have yelled right into his face.

Mike skids to a stop by the stove, waiting expectantly. He looks normal, by which I mean not-high and not-drunk. Good.

"What … … want, Skylar?"

"You called me."

He and Cam are both looking at me like I've sprouted a second head. I am *definitely* overreacting.

"Miss click." He shrugs. "Anything else?"

Cam has left the room, calling something indistinguishable after one of his siblings. Or siblings' friends. Mike is waiting, leaning one shoulder against the wall.

"Nope, I'm good. Never mind."

"Cool."

It's when he turns to leave that I catch the barest hint of marijuana. Maybe I'm imagining things? My stomach clenches. *Please, don't let this be a repeat of last summer.*

Somehow, I manage not to let worry about Mike ruin the whole evening. Cam's parents set out a generous build-your-own sub buffet and we eat dinner spread across the back deck, with the crowd of pre-teens seated on the stairs and the rest of us at the dinner table. With the background chatter of Cam's siblings' friends (plus a breeze that seems determined to swell the minute someone tries to talk to me), I can't hear much.

Cam's mom waves one hand at me across the table, and then signs SORRY once she has my attention. Cam must have told her I don't know much ASL, because when she's sure I can see her lips, she says, "We'll eat inside tomorrow."

"It's no problem." I wave a hand in what is supposed to be a dismissive manner and almost fling my sub into Mike's lap. He ducks. I catch a glob of mayo on one finger and try not to blush. "I mean…thanks."

After the dishes are done and the sun is setting below the trees at the back of the property, Cam and I put a movie on, sprawled across the couch with my head on his lap. He puts the captions on, and I pull my hearing aids out, setting them gently on the coffee table. With his siblings talking in the other room, I can't hear the TV anyway.

I fall asleep halfway through the movie and wake up when Cam shakes my shoulder, pointing to his watch to show me the time.

"Okay," I mumble, snagging my hearing aids and stumbling up the stairs to bed. The lights are off, and when I bump into Mike's door, swinging it gently open, he's just a lump on the mattress, his phone screen lighting up his face.

"Hey," I mumble, rubbing my eyes with my free hand. "Wake me up in the morning, okay? To go running?"

I can't see his face and don't have my hearing aids in, so I don't bother waiting for a response. I crash into my own room, not bothering to turn the lights on, and black out almost immediately on top of the covers.

• ● •

When I wake up the next morning, sun streams bright through the curtains. Did I oversleep? Is Mike gone already?

I roll out of bed and haul on a pair of yoga pants, wrestling into a sports bra and tank top and slipping my hearing aids behind my ears before pulling my hair into a ponytail. Maybe I can catch him at the door.

But when I come downstairs, Mike is walking in, not out, collar hitched to the side, glued in place by the damp circle of sweat that bleeds down his chest.

"You ran without me?" I feel pathetic as soon as the words leave my mouth.

Mike looks up at me, slipping off his shoes. "Sorry, Sky. I tried to wake you."

Did he?

The kitchen looks like ours back home when everyone's trying to get ready for school: Cam's younger sisters are rummaging in the fridge while his parents pour coffee into travel mugs and reach over each other for spoons and sandwiches, everyone bumping hips and shoulders. Cam's mom winces and sticks her pinky finger in her mouth. Cam's dad spills coffee on the counter but can't reach the dish cloth to wipe it up. I can practically see Sara dropping her bowl of Cheerios or Aiden somehow managing to get a paper cut on the cereal box. My little twinnies would fit right in here.

I lean towards Mike so I don't have to raise my voice. "Where's Cam?"

Mike dodges an oncoming pre-teen and hops onto the step next to me. "Haven't seen him. But hey, I wanted to ask you something."

"What's up?" I turn my head so he's speaking directly into my hearing aid.

"Well, I—"

He pauses for such a long time that I have to glance at his face to make sure my batteries haven't died suddenly. He's not talking—just running his hand over his hair over and over, looking awkward.

"What is it?"

"It's this job I'm applying to," he says. "You know, for something ... ... this summer. There are some questions ... ... the application ... ... that I need your help ... ..."

"My help?"

He nods.

"What's the position?"

"Guitar teacher." His face kind of lights up when he says it.

"Like at home?" The first thing Mike did after university ended in April was come home and pick up all his old students again. I didn't even think about how much he'd miss them when we came to Golden Sound.

"Sort of." He hesitates. "It's a camp ... ... position. One ... ... the only ones ... ... found."

"Okay, cool."

"... ... a Christian camp."

My heartbeat skyrockets. Is this Mike's way of telling me he became a Christian and didn't know how to tell me? "Really?" I reach to pull him into a hug, but he steps back.

"... ... what I need your help with. Answering the questions ... . why I became ... Christian and stuff."

I'm about to ask why he *did* become a Christian, and when, but the sheepish look on his face stops me. "What do you mean?"

"Look, Skylar." He grips the banister with both hands, leaning close so I'll be sure to hear him. "We both know I'm not into religion, right?"

My heart crashes into my ribcage.

"But this is the only job I've found that isn't just standing be-hind a cash register for eight hours a day. I'd be good at it. You know I would. I just need a little help."

Before I can answer, a hand slips around my waist from behind, and I jump, whipping my head around so fast my ponytail smacks Cam in the face. He winces.

"Sorry." I put an arm around him, my heart still pounding after all my yo-yo emotions about my brother. "Don't sneak up on me like that."

"I called your name." He glances down at the kitchen. "I see why you didn't hear me."

Mike mumbles something in our general direction and takes off, leaping up the steps two at a time before vanishing at the top of the hall.

"Where's he going?"

"Shower." Cam takes Mike's place, rests his chin on my shoul-der. "Want to grab breakfast?"

Cam's parents wave, his mom blowing us each a kiss before they leave for work, and then the last of the kids exits the kitchen, some disappearing onto the deck, some passing us on the stairs on the way back to their rooms.

"Bye," Cam says into the sudden silence, and I muffle a laugh.

"I can finally hear myself think," he says, stepping down off the stairs and into the kitchen.

"More importantly," I say, following him, "I can hear you."

Cam cocks his head, listening to something upstairs as he pulls open the fridge and hunts for the eggs. "It's Mike," he says when he catches my questioning glance. "Sounds like he's on the phone."

With the camp? A different job? Maybe working for a Chris-tian camp will encourage him to give Jesus a second chance. But is lying the way to do it? Before I can even open my mouth, a little smile tugs Cam's lips. "Skylar. Don't."

"What?" I turn toward the stove, fiddling with the dials to hide my blush. Cam is so onto me.

"Mike's a big boy." He says this right into my ear, so there's no chance I'll miss it. "He's doing okay. I promise."

"How do you know, though?" I nudge him away and take the bowl he passes me, cracking four eggs into it.

I see Mike enter the kitchen out of the corner of my eye, a shirt pulled halfway over his head and his phone pressed to his ear. He pinches the bridge of his nose like he's got a headache forming, nodding along to whoever's on the other end of the line as he shrugs the shirt over his shoulders.

"Okay," he says. He repeats this four times before hanging up. When he glances up from the phone and sees me watching him, he winces. "I have to go … ….. résumé to drop off today."

Beside me, Cam heats oil in the cast-iron skillet.

"Want me to drive you?"

Mike shakes his head. "You guys have fun. Save the library. Whatever you were going to do. I'll be back later." He turns to leave without waiting for a response.

"Where all are you going?"

He must not hear me, because the door slams shut and doesn't re-open. Agh.

Beside me, Cam pours the beaten eggs slowly into the skillet. I slump into a seat at the kitchen table and pillow my chin on my forearms.

Cam bumps my elbow gently, so I look back up.

"I have something that will cheer you up." He grins, gesturing for me to pass him the salt.

"What is it?" I force away all thoughts about Mike. I can deal with him later.

"I'm still thinking about doing something special, just the two of us. Like a real date, not just a movie night."

"What do you have in mind?" I grab two plates from the counter, and Cam scoops scrambled eggs onto each one.

"Aha!" He wiggles the spatula in my direction. "It's a secret."

"Well, then why'd you bring it up?"

"I'm creating suspense." He dodges the napkin I throw at him, laughing. Then he slides into the seat next to mine and passes me a fork.

"These eggs look amazing, by the way." I'm just raising a forkful to my mouth when I realize he's speaking, hands folded, eyes closed. He hasn't noticed me. For a moment, I have no idea what he's doing.

Then I realize he's praying. Oops. Why do I always forget the before-mealtime prayer? I shoot up a prayer of my own, hoping God will forgive me the other few hundred times I've forgotten over the past year.

The first few bites of breakfast taste like ash. Cam doesn't seem to notice, looking relaxed as he takes bite after bite, washing it all down with orange juice. He's lucky to live in a Christian family who all goes to church together. Who doesn't ask for explanations if you bow your head at the dinner table. Who doesn't raise their eyebrows when they catch you reading…let alone reading the Bible.

It's hard to be a Christian alone.

"Ready to go?" Cam holds out his hand for my empty plate. Our fingers brush when I pass it to him, and the realization fills me, warm and deep: I'm not alone anymore.

"Where are we going?"

"The library?" He turns his head as he slots plates into the dishwasher, making sure I can see his face. "Ana left me a key. We can take stock … come up with a plan of action." He looks so determined as he says this, the line of his jaw like a slab of rock. Strong and sure. "No need to start packing yet."

And yet…his fingers reach for the band of his wristwatch, which has cracked almost through, the leather worn away to almost nothing where it has been bent back and forth, twisted viciously, in a way that doesn't fit with the serenity of Cam's expression.

When he catches my glance, he shoves his hand into his pocket. Was he this flushed a few minutes ago? Maybe the heat from the stove is coloring his face a deep shade of pink. Or maybe it's something else.

"Ready to go?" He brushes past me, hands in his pockets, that blush high in his cheeks, pinkening his ears.

I hesitate, but when he turns, I wonder if I've imagined it.

"Skylar?"

"Are you okay?" I glance down at his wrist, sure he'll catch my drift.

He puts his hands in his back pockets instead, where I can't see them. His lean against the counter looks casual, but he hasn't given me an answer.

"Why do you ask?"

"Your watch." I hold out my hand for it, and after a moment, he places his wrist in my hands. I pull the leather back, unbuckle the watch, and lift it gently away from his arm. It's left a red mark, the buckle pressed deeply into his skin. "See?"

"I guess … … little tight." He mumbles, chin ducked like a little boy who knows he's about to get in trouble. I can barely hear him.

"Doesn't that hurt?"

"Skylar, it's fine." He rubs his wrist firmly with the fingers of his opposite hand, trying to smooth the skin. It looks angry and puckered where the blood is flowing back into the compressed skin. Small purple bruises dot the edges of the buckle imprint, like in his haste to loosen and tighten it, he's caught his skin in between without even caring.

"Cam…"

"Let's go, Sky." He reaches for the watch, but I pull it away from him and slide it into my pocket. He doesn't protest, just runs his hand along the back of his head, scratching almost absently, like he needs something to do with his hands.

I wait for him to break the moment, hoping he'll talk to me if I don't push him into it, but he doesn't say anything. Just opens his mouth, closes it again, and gestures questioningly toward the front door.

"Okay." If he doesn't want to talk about it, fine. But the weight of the watch in my pocket worries me; I can't stop thinking of those bruises in the tender place on the inside of his wrist. "Just give me a minute to change."

Cam doesn't speak again until we're in the car, seat belts on, radio turned down and fans on low. Sweat beads down my back in the hot car, but it's either AC or communication, so I just lean away from the seat and bear it.

"So," says Cam, slowly. I don't think he knows what to say. I don't, either. Cam is usually the level-headed one. The honest one. The annoyingly wise one. I'm not sure what to do now that there's something going on with *him,* and I don't think he knows how to handle it, either.

"It's just stress," he says, backing down the long driveway. "Honest, Sky. With the library...it's been a lot."

"Why didn't you tell me?" I run my thumb along the worn edges of the watch, the face cool and scratched against my skin.

He makes the turn onto the road. "It's ... ... stressful time. I didn't want you to worry the way you do—" He falters, but I know we're both thinking about Mike. "When I'm fine."

"But you're not *fine.*" I gesture to the marks on his wrist.

"That was an accident." He glances down at it, winces at the sight. "It happened yesterday. My skin pinched between the buckle. No big deal."

"Is it just the library? Or is it something else?" I'm thinking about school, wondering if something happened that he didn't tell me about.

Cam pulls the car over scarcely a kilometer away from his house, cresting gently to a stop on the soft shoulder. "Skylar. Look at me." He puts the car in park and reaches for my hands, setting his bruised wrist against my cheek.

I look at his lips instead of his eyes, desperate to catch every word.

"I'm not Mike." He squeezes my fingers. "I'm not going to do something dumb, or dangerous, or self-destructive. You don't … … worry about me. Okay?"

"Okay." I lean forward and kiss him across the center console, the gnawing feeling in my chest easing somewhat. Cam and I seem to slide into the same roles, no matter what the situation: him comforting me has been normal for us since the very beginning. Just like me worrying about Mike hasn't changed since last summer.

I shake myself away from worrying about Mike—what good has it done me so far?—and slip the watch into the cupholder between us, for Cam to retrieve later. "Let's go save a library."

Cam rests his hand on top of mine and pulls back out into traffic. "Sounds like a plan."

I lean my head against the passenger window and watch him drive, soaking in all the details of being in the actual same space as him instead of trying to make sense of him over a video call. He taps his fingers gently against the gear shifter, elbow resting on the inside of the car door so he can hold the wheel with one hand.

He's lost weight since last summer, but he's clean-shaven and his hair still sticks up in the center, just like it used to. That same easy smile spreads across his face when he catches me looking.

"Every … … okay?"

I reach across the console and twine my fingers with his. "It's the best."

He squeezes my hand, still smiling. I try not to think about leaving again at the end of the summer. I'm here now. I'm here for two whole months. I want to be totally here that entire time. Not thinking about going home again.

The fields are golden, the sky is blue, and Cam's hand swallows mine, my small fingers poking out between his long ones. And I mean it. This is the very best I can imagine.

In just a few short minutes, the speed limit drops, and Main Street shops come into view. Cam pulls into the library parking lot, which is empty except for a little girl in the corner, learning how to ride her bike.

"All right?" Cam flips the keys around his finger, a wrinkle I don't recognize between his eyebrows.

I unbuckle, grinning. I can't wait to get inside. "Let's do this."

At first, it seems to be going reasonably well. We change the window display to show tall stacks of summer reads, prop up a "closed for now" sign by a beach ball, and post a SAVE THE LIBRARY petition to the glass. Even though we don't know where to send the signatures yet.

Cam turns suddenly beside me, shading his eyes to glance across the street. "Yes?"

I spin, accidentally tearing a corner off the petition. I can tape it back down. No one will even notice.

A white-haired lady jogs across the street, knitting needles poking out of the rattan handbag hooked over her arm. I can see now that she's calling out to us, one hand waving, her voice lost to the wind. Only when she's standing on the sidewalk in front of us, one manicured hand pressed over her heart, can I finally hear what she's saying.

"... ... true? ... ... save the library?"

"We're going to try." I gesture at our half-taped-up petition, ripped corner and all.

"I'll sign!" Before I can hand over the sharpie resting on the windowsill, she's brandishing a pen. "Am I the first?"

Even Cam and I haven't put our names down, yet.

"Thanks, Beth." Cam must know her.

Beth writes her name down, tucks her pen back into her bag, and then pats it. "The knitting club has been having trouble finding a new place to meet now that the library's closed. I'll send the girls over to sign, too."

"Thank you." I can already imagine the names stretching onto a second page. Maybe we should put another one up, just in case.

"And who's this?" Beth turns her gaze to me. "Are you the sweet girl that worked here last summer?"

I nod, saved from having to admit I don't remember this woman when Cam puts an arm around my shoulders. "This is my girlfriend, Skylar."

My inability to hear her response has nothing to do with my hearing aids and everything to do with the fact that Cam's words are ringing loud and clear in my mind. He's never said it out loud before. Well, not in my presence anyway.

"... lovely to see you again," she says, patting my arm. "Well, now I've gone and made myself late for my knitting ladies." She raises a hand in farewell, turning to glance both ways before crossing the street again.

"See you on Sunday," calls Cam after her, and she blows him a kiss, continuing on her way down the street.

"Nice lady." I smack a piece of tape over the torn edge of the poster before Cam can turn and see it.

"She is," he agrees, looking hopeful.

Then, just as I'm pressing my thumb to the last piece of tape, Cam resting his chin on my shoulder as he watches, his phone rings. I can feel it vibrating against my hip, his pocket pressed to mine, and I feel his soft exhaled groan as he steps back and takes the call.

"Ana?" Her name, in his surprise, snaps cleanly out into the air between us.

The AC unit roars to life, churning a steady layer of noise over the rest of his conversation. I watch his face, gauge the temperature of the conversation by the lowering of his brows and the way his fingertips reach for his wrist, tremble harmlessly against the bare skin, and then immigrate to the back of his head, where he scratches absently again, like it's all for show. Just for something to do.

"What is it?" I ask when he pulls the phone away from his ear, but he shakes his head, lifts it up again.

"Hello?" A faulty connection. "... ... still there?"

The rest of the conversation is brief, Cam's frown firm and pronounced even though his lips say things like *that's nice* and *good to hear*. Something has gone wrong, even if everything else in the phone call is right.

I straighten books needlessly in the front display, giving up on any attempt to hear or lip-read. Even if this conversation had captioning, I'm pretty sure I'm on the less interesting half of the phone. It's Ana's words that hold the real answers here.

I'm reaching for one last book when I feel Cam's arms slip around me, his head coming to rest against the back of my neck. He sighs, breath hot against my skin.

"Cam?" I try to twist, to see him more clearly, but his face is buried against me. "What's wrong?"

He shakes his head, sucks in a deep breath, and then lifts his head so his chin is resting on my shoulder. "Ana's great," he says, and I know he must be feeding out the good news first. "She found a place ... ... job. She's been seeing a lot of Sophia and Eva."

"And?" I can't bring myself to act satisfied when I know there's more going on.

"And she ... ... about ... demolition." He sighs again.

I pull free and turn to face him. "I've been thinking about that. I bet we could still change their minds."

"How?" He looks tired, faint purple shadows under his eyes. "If they've already allocated funding? Signed the documents?"

"If we make a big enough fuss, they'll just re-allocate it." I hope this is true. "We can get more signatures on the petition. Send it to the mayor or something. Have a parade. If we can get enough people involved, they'll have to listen to us. They literally have another location option. Even if it seems less convenient, we can make *this* location look like a huge hassle if we protest enough."

Cam doesn't say anything. I grab his hand. "Right?" When he

still doesn't reply, I give it a little shake. "Come on, Cam. We can do this."

He doesn't believe me. I see him take me in, my own determined expression, hard grip on his hand. Maybe he replies because he doesn't know how to refuse. Maybe because he wants to believe I'm right. Or maybe because he sees something in me that gives him hope. But after a painfully long moment (or five), he nods.

"Okay. We'll give it a shot."

Chapter
SIX

Mike

FOR THE NEXT FEW DAYS, EVERY TIME MY PHONE BUZZES, I EXPECT ERIC. Sometimes, I don't even bother picking it up. Finally, after a new threatening text every few hours, I block his number. Problem solved.

An unknown number is calling me now, almost a week after I last saw Eric. I wish I didn't have to answer it. My laptop is open with a tab pulled up on each of the Golden Sound social media pages. We're up to almost a hundred followers on each, and I'd much rather keep drafting new posts than talk to whoever's on the other end of the line. If I'd just managed to study a little harder before final exams…

Just in case, I take the call.

"Is Micah there?" It's a girl's voice. I was expected a telemarketer. I'm so surprised I almost forget to reply.

I clear my throat. "Um, yes. This is he."

"Hi!" She sounds preoccupied, her voice coming from far away like she's put me on speakerphone. "This is the Golden Sound Adventure Camp calling about your application to be a guitar teacher. Do you have a minute?"

"Sure." I straighten in my seat, like she can see me. "I mean, yes." The answers I filled in the application must have worked. Thank Google—and Skylar, who sat me down last night and inundated me with details about God's love until I was breaking the character limit on all fields.

"Okay, great!" On the other end of the line, keyboard keys clack. "We liked your résumé—"

Thank goodness for my guitar students back home. I wouldn't be eligible for any positions other than cashier without them. And since I can't exactly use McDonald's as a reference, even those prospects are kinda iffy.

"—and we'd really like you to come in for an interview."

I take my phone away from my ear and put the camp representative on speaker so I can text Skylar.

Interview at Golden Sound Adventure Camp

She texts back almost instantly. *Yay!!!!!*

Thanks for your help

She sends a trail of smiley face and thumbs-up emojis in response. *You're crushing it!*

100 followers on the social media platforms, I text back. It's a day for celebration.

!!!!!!!!!!!!

"Hello?" The girl on the other end of the line sounds worried. "Micah?"

"Um, yes." I look up the address on Google Maps. "An interview sounds great." It's on the other side of Golden Sound, which means I'll have to drive through town to get there.

"Wonderful!" More keys clicking. "We have openings this afternoon and tomorrow, if you're available on such short notice." She sounds almost apologetic. "We've been having trouble finding someone."

I hear myself mumble an agreement. Maybe I'll stop and see Aunt Kay on the way back.

"Great! We'll see you in a few hours."

"Have a nice day." I hang up and open my messaging app again.

Sky. Interview this aft

In less than five minutes, she bursts through the door, arms full of...clothing?

"Mike! This is the best!" She throws the clothes, which must be Cam's, down on the bed. "I'm going to help you get ready, okay?"

"Sky, I have clothes—" But she's not looking at me, too busy rifling through the shirts on the bed. Cam wanders in after her, but leans against the doorframe instead of coming in.

"It's a kids' camp, right?" She opens the closet and shoves my hangers around before holding up a navy-blue blazer—the only one I own—and frowning slightly.

Like I'm going to wear a blazer to a camp interview.

"Mike?"

I nod. "But, you know—"

"This is too much," she declares, tossing it onto the bed, where it falls in a heap and begins wrinkling immediately. I scoop it up off the bed and smooth out the lines in the fabric. Maybe it was too optimistic to even bring it, but I thought it would be better to be prepared. What if I'd landed some sweet summer position at a local business? In my dreams, maybe. I hang the blazer back up in the closet.

Skylar has a hanger on each finger, half of the shirts mine and half belonging to Cam. She promptly discards half of each, tossing polos and button downs and plain old T-shirts to the bed, where Cam and I collect what belongs to us and retreat, well out of the way of her process.

"This one!" she declares at last, holding up a plain blue button down. "It's clean and classy, interview-style, but not, like, *too* dressed up."

"Thanks." I take it from her and lay it carefully—flat—down on the bed. "Okay, I think I'm good."

She stares at me. "We haven't done pants yet! Or shoes!"

Cam laughs openly from the doorway. I bet Skylar told him about the social media success. She doesn't hear—or maybe just chooses not to turn around. It's hard to tell.

"I only brought jeans," I tell her. "And khakis. And I have one pair of dress shoes. I think I'm good."

She looks a little disappointed, brushing stray hair out of her face. "Okay. Let's see the whole thing, then."

"You want me to put it all on?" I glance over her shoulder, hoping Cam will help. He steps backward out the doorway, still grinning, and disappears into the hall.

Smart.

"Yes!" Skylar folds her arms. "You want this job, don't you? Best foot forward, like Dad always says! Dress to impress!"

"Yes." But suddenly, I'm second-guessing my ability to lie about yet another thing. In an in-person interview, no less. Was this the biggest mistake ever?

"Okay then." She presses the shirt into my chest. "Go change. And did you bring any ties?"

I stare at her. "Sky. Come on. There's no way I'll need a tie for a camp interview."

"Okay, okay." Her small hands push me firmly toward the hallway. "Go change. No tie. I surrender."

• ● •

After Skylar formally approves of my interview outfit, after the shirt is ironed, just like my dad taught me, after I've applied cologne and made sure my shoes are relatively clean, there's still an hour left before I have to leave for the interview. Skylar and Cam have gone into town, Cam's parents are still at work, and I'm alone with my thoughts. Trying to think Jesus-y things to myself so I sound more authentic in the interview. Trying to rehearse my answers so if they ask about my work experience, I don't bring up the McDonald's job.

Alex's face pops to the front of my mind, tears rolling down her cheeks as she says *I didn't do it! Please believe me! It wasn't me.* Dang. That's exactly what I *don't* need in my head right now.

I pace the floor, checking my phone to see how quickly the time is passing. It drags, Alex's face seared across my memory. Finally, half an hour early, I escape to the car. I open Google Maps and plug in the camp address, intending on taking as many wrong turns as possible to add minutes to my ETA so I don't show up painfully early.

I take the first turn I can that directs me away from Eric's house, but I think about it anyway. Even after the entire town of Golden Sound is behind me, I can't stop thinking about what we did last summer. Seeing Eric again brought it all back. The tiny whisper that says, "Who might find out about it?"

When I turn down the long country driveway that leads to the camp, I'm sweating. The blue button-down Skylar selected for me is soggy and cool under my armpits, even though I turned the AC on high and drove the last few kilometers with my elbows up and out to the side like a big, awkward bird.

It's too late to do anything about this now. I park the car, tuck my résumé underneath my arm, and crunch up the gravel pathway to the camp office. There's a girl sitting behind a computer who looks up at me when I enter, smiling politely while she waits for me to say something. Was she the one on the phone earlier?

"I'm here for an interview," I tell her, trying not to think about her blue eyes, the way one curl of hair is lying just below her collarbone, the way her T-shirt sits across her slim shoulders—but too late, I'm sweating again. For a different reason. "For a guitar teacher, I think?" Why did I say that? I know what this interview is for.

"They didn't tell me about an interview," she murmurs, fingertips clacking against the ancient keyboard. So, not the same girl.

Not nearly as excited. "Oh. Wait. Yes, I've got it here." She stands, offering me a broad grin. I try to read her name badge but can't quite make it out. "Come on back." She leads me down a hallway and points to the first door on the right. "Go on in when you're ready. Okay?"

I nod my thanks and wait for her to disappear back down the hallway before I knock on the door.

"Come in!" At least whoever it is *sounds* cheerful enough.

When I push open the door, a grey-haired woman rises to greet me, another smile on her face. "Mike, right?" She's wearing jeans and a camp shirt, and I'm glad I ignored Skylar's suggestion of a tie.

"Yes." I set my résumé on the table and run my palms down the backs of my thighs. I'm still sweating. "Thanks for, uh, having me here today."

"Of course, of course." She leafs through my résumé and cover letter, motioning toward the chair beside me. "Please, sit."

I do as she says, trying to keep my back away from the chair in case I start sweating on that, too. She questions me about my guitar experience—why didn't I think to bring mine with me to-day?—and asks if I have my police check.

Finally, she sits back, smiling. "Mike, you seem like a good fit for our program."

I resist the urge to wipe my hands on my pants again. "Thanks."

"We ask the older students to bring their own guitars from home, but we start the younger kids on ukuleles. Do you have experience teaching ukulele, as well?"

I nod. I start the really tiny kids on ukes, too.

"Perfect." She folds her hands on the table. "Now. Because we're a Christian camp, I'd love to hear you talk a little bit about your own faith in God."

I clear my throat. This is it. What would Skylar say? "Well." I clear my throat. "It's relatively new for me. I grew up in an, um, atheist home."

She nods encouragingly.

"But then last summer I went through some stuff—" this part, at least, is totally true. "—and just really felt overwhelmed by the love of God." That's the exact phrase Skylar used. I don't really know what it means, but it earns me a smile from the camp director that causes only a faint prickle of guilt to crawl up my spine.

"That's wonderful, Mike." She's actually beaming. "I'm so glad to hear it."

"Thank you." Is that the right thing to say? I force myself not to squirm.

"Now, as a guitar teacher, you won't necessarily have students asking you about your faith in God, but if they do, how will you respond?"

Woah. Didn't see this one coming. I lick my lips, trying not to look panicked. "I would just, uh, be honest with them, I think. Tell them it's kinda new for me. Probably try to point them back to the priest—" do they have priests at camp? No. What are the modern ones called? "—pastor. I meant the pastor if they had any really serious questions or concerns."

"I see." She studies me for a moment, thinking. "Mike, I'm really impressed with your résumé. And, as I said in the job posting, we haven't had any luck finding a teacher for the guitar sessions."

I nod like I know where she's going with this.

"So," she continues, "I'd be pleased to offer you the job."

I stand up and reach across the desk for her hand, heart pounding. *Thank you.* "Thank you, ma'am. I really needed this job."

She looks pleased. "Would you like to meet some of your students?"

Now? "Sure," I say. If I could just stop sweating.

I follow the woman down the hall again and into a large gymnasium. "Wait here," she tells me, weaving through groups of children seated on the ground, every so often reaching out to tap a child on the head or shoulder, beckoning them to follow her.

When she comes back to me, there are four children with her, all looking expectantly up at me.

"These four will be your first session," she tells me, resting a hand on one of the girls' heads. "You'll have an afternoon class, too, but they're having outdoor activities at the moment." She lists each of the kids' names for me, which fly through my head without stopping long enough for me to remember, and then sends them all back to their groups.

One little girl—the one she had her hand on—steps forward, hand extended. "Hello, sir."

I grip it awkwardly. Her fingertips are hard and calloused—like mine. "Hi. You don't have to call me sir." She reminds me of a female version of my little brother, Aiden.

"I'm Emily." She tucks her hands behind her back, still staring up at me. "I love playing my ukulele."

"Me too." I smile.

"I have my dad's old one," she says, eyes wide. "I play every day. Are you going to be my new teacher?"

"I think so." She's at that awkward height where you can't crouch or you're shorter than eye-level, but standing over her makes me feel like I'm looming. I put my hands on my knees and compromise with a lean, instead.

She jumps a little in place. "I like you. Are you coming back tomorrow?"

"Next week," says the woman who hired me, whose name I have also forgotten. "He starts on Monday, Emily."

She does a little hop again. "Bye!"

Before I can say good-bye, she's sprinting back to her group, skidding to a seat on her butt in the middle of the circle.

"Lovely," says the woman, smiling over at her before turning to look at me. "I think you'll fit in really well here." She begins walking back toward the office, so I follow her. "I'll send you home with some forms, and I'll have Lily call your references this weekend.

As long as you e-mail me a copy of your police check, you can start Monday."

"That would be great." I wait in the doorway of the office while she organizes the forms, sorting them all into a folder, which she passes over to me with a smile. "Thanks again for the job." I lift the folder awkwardly in salute. "I'm really looking forward to it."

She reaches for my hand and gives it a firm shake. "I have a feeling it's going to be my pleasure."

On my way out the door, I offer the girl at the front desk a smile, which she returns, and on the way back to the car, I'm starting to feel better. My palms are dry, the sun is warm on my face, and I have a job. Finally. And no sermon to accompany it. I half-expected they'd make me say some prayer with my right hand on a Bible, but they seem...chill. Like Skylar and Cam.

I slide behind the wheel, stick the key in the ignition, and pull my phone out of my pocket to make sure Skylar hasn't texted me. She hasn't, but Aunt Kay has.

Missing my favorite eldest nephew!

Crushed a job interview, I write back. *Be over in five*

See you soon. I burned a cake, but the icing is still good. I'll save you some.

And then she adds, *Did you tell your parents yet?????*
I turn my phone off and put the car in drive.

Chapter
SEVEN

Skylar

IT TURNS OUT, SAVING A SITE ALREADY MARKED FOR DEMOLITION IS JUST NOT as easy as I thought it was going to be. Cam and I spend days emailing all the local powers we can think of, writing to other local businesses in town, and gathering names for our petition. Which we still don't fully know how to organize.

"We're not going to let them win," I tell Cam every morning, and his own firm expression always greets me in return. Not this town. Not this time.

But on Saturday, after our first week of efforts has petered out and we're left waiting to hear back from all of our original messages, the whole thing starts to feel a little out of our league.

Cam's mom stacks a baking sheet high with breakfast sandwiches and leaves them in the oven on warm before leaning over Cam's shoulder to see what we're working on.

"How's it going, guys?"

"Slow," Cam says shortly, head ducked to see the screen.

"But good, though." We have to stay positive. "We're just waiting for people to email us back right now. Nothing exciting."

She pulls up the seat next to Cam. "Do you need any help?"

"Yes," we both say in unison. I flash a grin at him.

"If you could get me the personal phone number of the board of directors in charge of this," says Cam, shaking his head, "that'd be great. I keep getting his voicemail."

"And his email has an auto-responder set," I add, pulling up the fourth *I am currently unavailable* message I've sent to Trash this week. "Do you think he's ignoring us on purpose?"

"Probably not." Cam's mom tilts her head to one side. "At least, I hope he isn't. I'll talk to your dad and see if he knows where to find a better contact line." She gets up, pushing her chair in.

"Thanks, Mom."

"Thanks," I echo.

Cam pulls the laptop closer and bends over it again.

"So." I lean over, trying to get him to look at me. "While she looks into that, do you want to take the day off?"

He barely looks at me, squinting at the screen instead. "We can't take time off yet. There's a lot left to do."

"Come on, Cam." I try to wiggle an eyebrow. "You've been talking about going on a date, right?"

At last, he looks away from the computer. "I have, but—" He pauses for a moment, looking at me. "Maybe you're right."

"Aha!" I pump a fist in the air. For a second, I thought he was going to cancel the whole thing. Whew.

"I've got a few places in mind."

"I'd love that!" There are so many places we could go—a park, a hike, a long romantic walk on the beach—but by the look on his face, Cam has somewhere specific in mind.

"It'll be perfect." He opens a second tab, and then a third, leaning in close to the screen. "I'll find the nicest restaurant in town. We've never been on a real dinner date, you know."

"I know." I lean my head on his shoulder as he searches Yelp. "Hey, what about that one?" I point at a tiny restaurant inn that claims to have the best waffles in town.

Cam copies the link and opens a note on his computer, pasting the name and address down.

"What's the list for?"

"So we can keep track of our options." He opens the web page of a high-end fancy restaurant, where every table has candles and wineglasses and there are three spoons beside the plate. He pastes this down in the doc, too, and puts a little asterisk in the column next to it.

"That one's probably expensive." If last summer's anything to go off, Cam only makes minimum wage at the library in the summers, and probably less than that at the university library when he's away at school.

He shrugs, then turns to brush a kiss on my forehead, his eyes still on the screen. "You're worth it."

I grin, butterflies fidgeting in my stomach, and he smiles back.

"What about this?" He's opened another fancy restaurant with windows that face the water.

"Look!" I point to the corner of the page. "They have a bistro/café thing! We could go for lunch!"

"Let's do something extravagant." Cam copies down the bistro name. "I want to take you somewhere really special. Somewhere"—he winks at me—"perfect."

"A bistro could be perfect, too," I say, but mildly. He nudges my elbow like he thinks I'm kidding and goes on searching.

"I want to take you somewhere you'll remember forever."

This time I'm the one who bumps into him, thinking maybe I can lovingly knock some sense into him. "This whole summer is locked in my memories forever. So is last summer." Meeting Cam, mistaking him for a cowboy, grabbing the wrists of a boy I'd never met just to stop him from signing too fast. Hugging Anastasia across the counter. Tim Horton's muffins and raspberries and a whole carton of Rocky Road.

"Good." He seems utterly unfazed—and also unlikely to change his mind—so I rest my chin on his shoulder to inspect the latest website he's pulled up. It's yet another formal-wear type of venue, where you have to reserve a table, and I'll probably have to borrow a pair of Cam's mom's high heels.

"My parents have mentioned this one before," he says, grinning at me in a way that makes me forget everything. "They took us once a few years ago. The lighting is strong at the tables, so it'll be good for lip-reading. And my parents said they don't play background music any of the times they've been. And—"

He is so excited about this it hurts my chest a little. I kind of thought he was more wrapped up in the idea of the date than actually thinking about us. And it turns out he's been thinking about *me* this entire time.

"—the tables are super far apart, to make it 'private'"—he adds air quotes—"but that means there shouldn't be that much background noise from everyone else talking." He finishes, leans back in his chair, and waits for my opinion. He can't keep the smile off his face.

"It sounds perfect." And it does. Even if I have to wear high heels.

"Great!" He picks up his phone again. "I'll make a reservation. For tonight?"

"Sure."

He dials, presses the phone to his ear. Waits, drumming his fingers on the table. "Yes," he says, when someone picks up on the other end. "Please. For tonight."

I glance away, and when I look back, he's frowning. "None? Okay. Tomorrow?"

Uh-oh.

His frown deepens. "Really? That far in advance?"

The phone call ends shortly after, and Cam rubs the tips of his fingers into the soft skin of his eyelids. "They're fully booked," he says to me, his mouth a flat line. "I'm so sorry, Sky."

I shrug. "It's okay. There are lots of other places we could go."

Cam looks way too bummed out about this restaurant. "I just wanted it to be perfect," he says, flipping his watchband back and forth absentmindedly, yanking the band tighter and then undoing it completely and letting the watch fall onto the table. I wince when the glass face hits the wood, but the sound I'm expecting is swallowed, at the wrong pitch for my hearing aids to gather.

"Why does it matter so much?" I grab his hand. I can't stand to see him fiddling with the watch anymore. "We'll have fun. We always do."

He rests his head against mine. I can't see his face, but there's no rumble in his chest that says he's speaking, so I keep talking.

"Let's go somewhere normal." I close my eyes. "Someplace quiet and lovely and comfortable. Let's pick somewhere that looks like the kind of place we belong."

I pull back to see the half-smile that crosses Cam's face.

"Ana's going to be so disappointed her idea didn't pan out."

"You asked Ana for dating advice?"

He blushes. "I may have texted her. Just to get a few ideas. She told me, and I quote," He makes quotation marks with his fingers, "'Go big or go home.'"

He is so cute.

"I could see Ana liking something like that." Ana wears high heels and bows and makeup just to work at the library. I can picture her waltzing into a restaurant like that, curls piled high on top of her head, running a pink fingernail down the menu and saying, "Tell me about your specials, please," with a little wink to the waiter.

"I figured she'd know what to do. To make it really special." Cam holds the watch in his hand, fingers clenched closed over the face of it.

"We can make our own kind of special." I close my fingers over his. "Do you want me to pick the place?"

He shakes his head. "I'll think of something else. I've got kind of another idea already."

"Want to tell me about it?"

He grins. "Nope."

"A hint?"

He tugs the computer away from me, even though I didn't reach for it. "Absolutely not. This is going to be a surprise. A really good one."

I kiss his cheek. "I know it."

"Okay." He stands up, computer perched in his arms like a precious package. "I'm going to my room to finalize the details."

"What am I supposed to do?" I laugh at him, the way his hand cups the screen protectively.

"Look up more library stuff." He turns toward the stairs.

"You have my computer!"

He grins over his shoulder at me. "Go for a run? Be free! Have fun." Before I can tease him, he's halfway up the stairs. "Bye, Skylar."

I don't hear his bedroom door close, but the sight of him disappearing up the stairs has the same effect. What am I going to do now?

I do end up going for a run, the anticipation of our evening hanging over me. I want to know everything about what he's chosen, and why. I want to know what put that secretive look on his face.

When I jog in through the front door an hour later, the house is still empty, but there's a note tacked to the closet door.

Sky: is 7 good?

I don't know why he didn't just text me, but I peel off the sticky note and fold it into fourths. I'll slip it into the pocket of my suitcase later, so I can tack it to my bulletin board back home.

It's already almost five o'clock, so I dash up the stairs and start yanking clothes out of my suitcase, trying to find my favorite jeans and the one nice top I packed: a light green blouse with bell sleeves and a scoop neck. Not fancy enough for the restaurant Ana recommended, but perfectly *me* and perfect for whatever Cam has planned for tonight. I hope.

I take extra care washing and drying my hair, pinning it up into a bun instead of just braiding it like I usually do. Cam texts as I'm brushing on my mascara.

I knocked but you didn't hear. almost done?

I cap the mascara tube and yank the door open, arms spread. "Done! How do I look?"

His mouth doesn't fall open, but his eyes soften at the corners. He swallows, the Adam's apple that I never noticed before bobbing in his throat. "Absolutely perfect."

"Perfect," I echo, slinging an arm around his neck to give him a quick hug. "Are we leaving now?"

"We are."

We pass Mike in the hall. He's got his backpack slung over his shoulder and his guitar in hand, and he flashes us a thumbs-up when we go by.

"How's camp?" I grab his arm, pulling him to a stop before he can go into his room. "Mike?"

"It's good, Skylar." He actually grins at me, hefting the guitar with one hand. "Really good. The kids are great. It's a good job."

When is the last time he's offered this much information after such a simple question? Maybe things are finally starting to move. Maybe God is finally getting through to him. "That's awesome!"

Mike nods a greeting to Cam. "Have fun, guys."

I dance down the stairs and into the entryway, slipping my feet into the barely worn sandals I brought to wear to church. Cam seems happier, too, squeezing my hand as we fly down the country roads, humming to himself as he makes each turn. When we have to stop at the Golden Sound traffic light, he turns to me over the center console.

"You're going to like it." He grins. "I can't wait to see your face when we pull in."

I laugh, even though he's not being funny. I'm just so happy I have to let it out *somehow*. Even the library seems like a distant trouble with no bearing on tonight.

Eventually, after what feels like an eternity, Cam pulls into a small gravel parking lot overlooking the beach. The setting sun traces a path of liquid gold across the waves. "We're here."

"Where is it?" I scan the beach, looking for a restaurant.

"You'll see." Cam unbuckles. "Close your eyes, okay?"

"What?" I try not to frown. I hate closing my eyes—not being able to hear *or* see. "Do I have to?"

Cam considers, head tipped to one side. "Well, no. Nah. It's fine. Just wait here for a moment." He disappears around the back of the van, and I force myself to stare at the waves, even though I'm dying to look and see what he's doing.

When he reappears, he's got a backpack slung over his shoulders.

"What kind of restaurant *is* this?" I unbuckle and jump out of the car, crossing in front to hold his hand.

"Your favorite kind," he says. "I hope."

We walk a little way down the beach together, admiring the little cottages that back onto the water. And then, right when I think I've spotted a little restaurant with a patio, tiny string lights crossing over each table, Cam stops.

"We're here."

I'm still looking at the restaurant—it looks like the bistro from the web page—so I don't realize he's set the backpack down until I turn around.

"Surprise," he says, unzipping the backpack. "Welcome to the best restaurant in the whole world." He tugs out a blanket, which he unfurls and spreads across the sand.

"A picnic?"

The sun has turned the world to gold and set Cam's hair on fire. He looks concerned. "Is that okay?"

It's the best thing I can think of. I sit down on the picnic blanket beside him and accept the cutlery he passes me, spreading everything out on the blanket. "Cam. It's perfect."

The last thing to come out is the food, which is in a series of plastic containers I can't quite see through.

"What is it?"

Cam grins as he tugs off the first lid to reveal a stack of waffles, so warm they've left condensation beaded on the lid. "Breakfast for dinner."

The other containers hold strawberries, chocolate chips, chopped peanuts, and banana slices. Cam sets a bottle of syrup down on the blanket and hands me a can of whipped cream. "Bon appétit, Skylar."

I hold my plate out for a waffle, unable to keep the smile off my face. And then, neither one of us says anything, upending the containers over our plates, passing the syrup back and forth, and frothing whipped cream into peaks on our plates.

When I'm halfway through my second waffle, chewing through a blissful mouthful of whipped cream, Cam wipes his mouth with the back of his hand and waggles his fingers to get my attention.

"Do you like it?" He looks nonchalant, the fork and knife still held in his other hand, but something about his eyes looks open and hopeful. Like my little brother, Aiden, when he asks a question. I swallow, the sweet lightness of the cream still lingering at the corners of my lips, and grab his hand. "Yes."

If there was more to say, I'd say it, but I try to put everything I feel into the one word: the glory of the setting sun, the grit of the sand against my toes, the way my hair fell apart two seconds after we sat down and not a soul was here to see it. The waffles, the whipped cream, *him*. And not even so much as a breeze to move the waves and send feedback through my hearing aids.

The grin that splits his face says he understands completely.

Chapter
EIGHT

Mike

I TELL MYSELF I HAVE TIME TO STOP AT AUNT KAY'S AND MOW THE LAWN BE-fore work (if I skip my morning run, I don't even have to wake up any earlier) but I forget to calculate my aunt's personality into my schedule. After I step out of her shower with five minutes to spare, I take my time toweling off and getting dressed, only to find Aunt Kay leaning over a smoking stove with twice the amount of burners turned on as there are pots.

"I was heating those up!" she complains, when I reach over and turn half of them off.

"For what? A fire hazard?" I step into my shoes and reach for the door, but she calls me back.

"You aren't going to have any breakfast?"

"I packed extra for lunch." My phone buzzes with a notification on the Golden Sound Instagram. It hasn't gained any new followers since it crested 100. In fact, I see when I open the app that it's actually dropped to ninety. And the DM that lit up my phone is from one of those spam accounts that only sends messages saying *DM for collab.* I delete it.

Aunt Kay raises an eyebrow. "Extra?"

"I *did.*" But I sit down anyway, closing the app and checking the time underneath the table. I have to leave in exactly two minutes, or I'll be late.

"Just let me put a plate together." Aunt Kay disappears into the living room for some reason, but when one more minute ticks down and I poke my head through the doorway, I can't see her.

"Aunt Kay?" Nothing. "I have to leave soon." I double-check Instagram. I put up a new post yesterday, but it's only gotten 4 likes. Twitter is even worse. Another minute ticks by before my aunt comes back, flushed, but triumphant.

"I knew I put that thermos somewhere."

To her credit, she pours me coffee and packs me a Tupperware container of French toast in thirty seconds flat, but even though I sprint down the deck steps and across the driveway to my car, I know it won't be enough.

I call a goodbye over my shoulder, leap into the driver's seat, and pull out without buckling my seatbelt. I've only driven a few streets when I realize I forgot to put the camp address into my GPS, so I mutter a curse under my breath and pull over, fingers fumbling with the screen once the car is parked safely on the side of the road. I *hate* being late for things. But I'm going to have to deal with it today.

At last, with the address typed in correctly, I throw the car into drive and peel off down the road, hoping to make up a few minutes as I go. But I get stuck behind some old lady doing ten under the speed limit, which means I actually *lose* time. I swallow back a few choice words. It's not her fault.

When I finally get to work, Lily is standing by the door, peering anxiously into the parking lot like she expects me to materialize out of thin air.

I put the car in park, slam the driver's door, and lock it from the fob as I jog toward the doors. "I'm really sorry I'm late."

"There you are!" Relief crosses her face, and she wooshes out the breath she'd been holding. "I was just thinking we'd have to split them up into the other small groups. Thank goodness you've saved me from that organizational nightmare." She has every right to be angry with me, but for some reason she's still smiling.

"I got lost." I follow her into the building. My phone buzzes in my pocket with a message from a number I don't recognize.

"No problem. Happens to the best of us." Lily throws a totally distracting smile over her shoulder. It's almost enough to take my mind off my problems. But not quite.

Blocking my number was a mistake. Spot me $50 and we'll call it even

I stumble over a rough edge in the carpet and almost trip, slipping my phone back into my pocket. Why is Eric desperate enough to text me from someone else's phone? Doesn't he have anyone else to ask for money? "Are they in our breakout room again?" I thought he'd give up if I didn't pay up the first time. How far will he take this?

Lily nods her head, her hair twisted in two long braided ropes, like whatever Skylar does with her hair. It looks nice. "Yes, but we've moved you across the hall, just for the day. There was a kid-related mess a few minutes ago in your original room." She wrinkles her nose.

I don't ask.

"Here," she says. "I'll show you."

I follow her down the hall, peering into each doorway as we pass. Last week, I was so focused on learning the ropes that I actually didn't even bother to look around. Now I see that some of the younger kids are doing arts and crafts, and the older ones are either reading quietly, playing board games, or playing instruments in small groups. Some of the rooms stand empty, with just a few backpacks to show that there were ever kids there at all.

"They're outside," says Lily, catching me looking. "Archery and stuff like that."

I can't help feeling a little impressed. That actually sounds kind of fun. "So you don't just sit around singing 'Kumbaya' all day?" I realize way too late that I've picked the wrong audience for this joke.

She grins. "My boyfriend asked the same thing when he first stopped by."

The mention of a boyfriend kills the conversation. Good to know. No flirting allowed.

"This one's yours." She stops at the first classroom on the right and motions to the open door.

"Great, thanks." I'm thankful for the guitar case that separates us. "See you later."

"Good luck!" She pokes her head into the room, waves at the kids, and then heads back to her desk.

When I enter the room, the kids' heads swivel to look at me, all of them bright-eyed and blinking inquisitively. I try to imagine them all as Aiden and Sara. It doesn't totally work.

The girl from the other day, Emily, thrusts her hand into the air.

"Yes?" I set my guitar case to the side, to use with the older kids—the ones with bigger hands—in afternoon session.

"Are we going to play a guitar? Today?"

"We'll probably start with ukuleles." I glance around the room. There's a whole wall full of ukes behind the kids, so finding an instrument for everyone shouldn't be a problem.

"I have a question too!" A tall boy in the back stretches his arm up high, wiggling every finger. "Are you married?"

All the kids giggle.

"No, I'm—"

"How old are you?"

Clearly, teaching a room full of fourth-graders is going to be a little different than the one or two students I normally teach at a time.

"Okay, maybe we can do some questions later—"

The kids ignore me.

"Did my hamster go to heaven when it died last year?"

They're not even raising their hands anymore.

"Why don't you ask your—"

A little girl turns to the hamster-owning kid and says in a booming voice, "My dad says heaven is only for people."

The hamster kid looks horrified.

"Who wants to play a ukulele?" I bellow it into the room, and everyone turns to stare at me. Except hamster kid. He's definitely crying.

The dark-haired girl—Emily—raises her hand. "I do!"

I spy an opportunity. "Everyone go grab a uke from the wall." I add, "Carefully, please," but it's too late: the stampede has begun. In the chaos, I crouch next to hamster-owner's chair. He's wiping his nose on the hem of his shirt. "Hey, buddy."

In the corner, two girls appear to be arguing over a pink ukulele. As long as they're not hitting each other over the head with it, I guess it's fine.

Hamster boy sniffs. "I'm not crying."

Why aren't there Kleenex boxes in here? "It's cool, man." What am I supposed to say now? "You know, I think your hamster is probably somewhere really awesome right now."

He sniffs again. "You do?"

I nod. "Definitely. He's probably running around, eating snacks, and running on his little wheel." Or whatever it is that hamsters like to do.

Hamster boy perks up. "Mr. Mike, do you know everything?"

Definitely not. "I know some stuff."

"Do you think my hamster is with Jesus now?"

Aw, dang it. How should I know? I need Skylar. "Yes." Do I sound confident enough? "I think Jesus loves your hamster."

The kid beams. And I shoot a quick text to my sister before getting the lesson started for the day.

•••

The morning session passes quickly—for the kids. Some of

them have never even *seen* a ukulele before and spend the whole session scrubbing their hand frantically against the strings. The ones who have played before stare out the window or whisper to their friends, bored. I pass out music books and try to teach. The older kids in the afternoon are better, and by the time their parents start showing up at the door, I think I'm finding my groove.

It's not until I settle in the car and turn my phone on to find another text from Eric (this one says *I'll go to the police*) that I first let the word *blackmail* sink in.

For a while, I could pretend it wasn't happening. Blackmail seems like the kind of thing that belongs in crime novels and detective shows, not something a couple of college kids stumble into while they're high out of their minds.

But here I am.

I pull into the bank parking lot and drive through the ATM, poking my card through the slot and withdrawing the $50 he asked for. I'll only do this once. Just to buy myself some time to think.

The ATM churns out a receipt, and I rip it free and drive away, rolling the window up as I let the car crawl through the lonely plaza on the edge of the highway. Maybe I should just tell Skylar now. What's the worst that could happen?

Her face pops into my mind, wide-open in shock, then crumpling as she listens. Then ironing out into determination and activism. *We can fix this*, she'd say. *I'll ask Cam, he knows someone who can help—*

I shake the vision away. I don't need my baby sister protecting me. I don't need her forcing Cam to come to my rescue again. I don't relish the thought of him hoisting my drunk self into the car at the end of this summer, too. Or calling a friend to walk me through the legality associated with last year's lies. My family is just starting to change their minds about me. I'd do anything not to jeopardize that.

When I came home at the end of the school year, Mom wasn't

surreptitiously sniffing my clothing every time I came in the door. Dad had stopped putting on his glasses and giving me long, hard looks every time we talked. I never found Skylar in my bedroom, guiltily claiming to be looking for her old T-shirt in my laundry. They were relaxed. They trusted me.

If I tell them about the robbery, that all goes away. Especially since I still haven't told them about school.

I remember how it felt to hold that stack of cash in my hand, all the sharp plastic edges of the money ready to slice into my palm. How Eric flashed me the thumbs-up, motioned for me to take some and put the rest back. He said everyone did it. Skimming off a big company like McDonald's was barely stealing at all. More like collecting an employee bonus. *And who needs it more, Mikey?* He'd slapped me on the back. *Some rich old CEO sitting in an office? Or a couple of poor high school students?*

Logic like that is hard to argue with when you're eighteen— just a year ago, and how could I have been so dumb?—and I didn't even feel bad about it. Not the first time. Not the second. But the third time I only took a twenty, and even that was only because I owed Eric. He'd spotted me a couple of beers at a party. A joint or two. I couldn't get the money from my parents. I *needed* it. But I swore there wouldn't be a fourth time.

And there wasn't. But only because we almost got caught.

My phone buzzes on the passenger seat. A text from Skylar. She backed me up with more info about that hamster question this morning, so I figure it's more God-talk. I don't pick it up right away, but it just keeps buzzing. I pull over by the side of the road and flick through my notifications.

> *Omg*
> *I saw eric*
> *He tore down a poster I was putting up*
> *He and Cam almost got into a fight*
> *(To be fair, idk if he meant to tear down the poster. I*

*flinched when he came up behind me so technically maybe
the poster was my fault)*
Where are you?? Mike answer me
Answer me!!!!

I press the call button before I realize it's no use. My hands shake as I fire off a text. I never thought he'd actually do something. I didn't think he was serious.

Are you ok
Skylar?

She responds almost immediately. *Yes, fine! Cam is here. Eric gone. Where are you?*

On my way home from work

I open my phone, navigate to my messaging app, and unblock Eric's number with trembling fingers so I can shoot him a text.

Don't take this out on Skylar. I hesitate before sending the next text. But I need to make sure he doesn't do anything else. *I have the money.*

Come over, he texts back almost immediately. Doesn't even mention Skylar. I wait a few more minutes to be sure neither he nor my sister is going to reply, and then I pull slowly out into traffic.

I follow the side roads back toward town, not even meaning to take the ones that lead past McDonald's. But there it is, the golden arches beaming through the late afternoon haze. By force of habit, I flick my signal on and pull into the turning lane, and by the time I realize what I've done, it's too late to merge back onto the highway.

Fists tight, I turn into the parking lot. I'm pulling a U-turn about as fast as I can, trying not to think about Alex, when I swear I see her walking through the doors. She always wore her hair in some kind of braid, and it swings behind her now as the glass door slaps shut behind her.

I throw the car into park and stare after her. Did they hire her back?

I remember the look on her face when the manager told her she was fired for stealing the money. How it felt like someone had dumped hot water all over me, starting with the top of my head. My palms had sweat so much I shoved them into my pockets.

• ● •

Alex's mouth had gaped open and shut, but she didn't say anything.

"You can go and get your things." The manager wasn't much older than me and a lot younger than Alex, who was somewhere in that murky age category where you know she's older than you but still younger than your parents. She had a kid.

"I didn't do it." She brushed the hair back from her face, eyes squeezed at the corners, like she was trying not to cry. "I really need this job. I would never steal. Please."

"—bacon cheeseburger—" Someone was trying to order, but I couldn't type a thing into the computer with my hands in my pockets. And I wasn't about to take them out.

"Here, let me." Eric shoved me roughly aside and finished the transaction. I was still watching Alex, who had started crying.

The manager glanced back, tugging at the neck of his shirt, his name badge half unclipped and flopping to the side. He looked like the kind of person who wanted to go home and game for a few hours instead of firing single mothers who didn't own their own car, had no one to call, and would probably be taking a taxi home if she could find one to pick her up. They're not plentiful in small towns like this one.

I did it. I opened my mouth, stepped forward, got one hand out of my pocket to get the manager's attention, but just couldn't find the courage to actually say the words yet.

Eric grabbed my arm. He spun me around, knocked me into

the counter like he was trying to get me to focus on the next cus-
tomer, and when they stepped forward to order, he hissed in my
ear, "Don't be stupid."

When I had looked up again, Alex was just a pale figure standing in the window, a braid and a backpack waiting for a ride home
in the dark. The manager had gone back into his office. The cus-
tomer got her hamburger. I resigned the next week.

But it still wasn't enough.

The alcohol had helped with the forgetting. But every morning,
more painful than the hangover were the memories.

As if urged on by my thoughts—the most time I've spent
thinking about this since last summer—a faint headache blooms
behind my right eye as I put the car in park and get out. All I want
to do is go home. But this is my chance to get ahead of whatever
narrative Eric has in mind.

I can go in there right now, apologize, set the record straight
and break the hold he has on me once and for all.

Gravel crunches under my feet as I cross the parking lot, my
step quickening as I approach the doors, thinking about the braid.
If they'd hired Alex back, they knew it was a mistake. Maybe Eric
gave his half of the money back. Told them some other story. Telling the truth now will be easy—they might not even care. It was
last summer, right?

The girl brushes past me on my way in, her long hair smacking
against my shoulder as she ducks out the door. Even as I scan the
restaurant, hoping to see Alex's face, I know I won't find her. I've
made a mistake, lured inside by hope and naiveté.

The cashier, chin in hand, watches me from behind the counter.
"Help you?" She drops the words in between chews of bubble gum,
looking bored enough to die.

Shelby. From last summer. I remember her from one of Eric's
parties. I think. Some of those parties are hard to remember.

I know the moment she recognizes me because she takes her
chin out of her hand and stands up, eyebrows narrowing. "Mike?"

I could still do it. Still ask for the manager. Explain about last summer. Ask if they know what happened to Alex.

"Do you remember me?"

I nod. "Can I have a coffee?"

She looks taken aback. "Hot or iced?"

"Iced." My palms are sweating again. I'm going to do this. "Shelby, I—"

My phone buzzes inside my pocket. Eric or Skylar? And suddenly I could name a million reasons why this is a bad idea.

She rings me in, cocks her head, and waits for me to continue.

"Good seeing you again." I snatch the coffee off the counter, duck my head, and walk back to the car.

Chapter
NINE

Skylar

ON MONDAY MORNING, I CAN'T WAIT TO GET TO THE LIBRARY. I FIGURE AFTER a whole weekend of our petition being taped to the glass, after that lady—Beth—and her knitting group show up and bring all of their friends, we're sure to have signatures.

"Right?" I lean my forehead against the bathroom door, talking to Cam even though I know I won't hear him if he says anything back. "It's been two whole weekend-days full of tourists and stuff. Aren't you excited?"

The bathroom door opens. Cam tugs on one of my braids. "Sure, Sky ... ... be great."

I don't need my ears to tell me his tone falls flat. His concerned expression is doing a great job of communicating that to me all on its own.

"Come on." I follow him down the stairs and out to the car, jamming my feet into sandals and double-checking that my hearing aids are behind my ears. I even remembered spare batteries today. "Today's going to be a good day. I can just tell."

Cam nods, but he's quiet all the way into town. By the time he parks the car in front of the library, his nervousness has rubbed off on me. My heart is pounding, knee jiggling up and down in the passenger side. Even from here, I can tell the petition isn't *full*. But there is something written down. I think.

"I'll go check while you park." Without waiting for a response, I undo my seatbelt, throw the car door open, and jump out while Cam pauses so he can parallel park in the too-small Main Street parking spot. I glance across the street—no traffic—and then sprint to the door, eyes trained on the petition.

Not one or two but *twenty* names, phone numbers, and email addresses track their way down the list. In just a weekend!

When Cam joins me, his eyebrows raised, I throw my arms around him. "We have to celebrate!"

He gives me a squeeze. "I guess we … …?"

"Ice cream?"

He laughs. "Now? At nine in the morning?"

I tug the keys out of his hand and unlock the doors myself, my heartbeat soaring through my veins. Everything is going to work out. "I'll go down the street and get some Rocky Road."

He follows me inside, flicking on the overhead lights. "Sounds … … me."

● ● ●

We eat ice cream straight out of the carton, sitting cross-legged on the floor, just like old times. Cam looks lighter than he has since I got here. Together, we upload the names to our online petition and start drafting another email to the mayor. Cam eats all the marshmallows out of the tub of ice cream, and I dig for the nuts. It's the new beginning we've been waiting for.

When we show up on Tuesday, I expect to see more names on the window petition. When there aren't any, I think surely on Wednesday. Or Thursday. By Friday, Cam has stopped looking, just ducking his head to unlock the front door, the muscles in his arms pulled taut. We don't bother checking on Saturday.

I toss prayers to God like pennies into a fountain, but nothing changes. At least, nothing I can see. Am I doing this all wrong? Discovering that God loves you is not the same thing as learning how to love Him back. At all. I know better than anyone that God doesn't answer prayers the way you expect Him to...but is it wrong to ask, anyway? Is it wrong to ask Him for this?

I'm still thinking about it on Sunday morning as we stand in church, the congregation singing words to songs I don't know and praying when I least expect it. We took the petition down yesterday, after several days with no new signatures, and the window display looks forlorn and abandoned without it. No matter how high we stack books, we can't create the illusion of use. The lights are off. Dust gathers faster than we can vacuum it away. The Golden Sound Public Library looks old, lost, and forgotten. No matter what we do.

The congregation sits abruptly, and I fall into my seat a half-second too late, glad I had my eyes open. Cam seems totally engrossed as the pastor steps to the front, mic in hand. I asked Mike if he wanted to come this morning—he's been texting me questions all week, probably so he knows what to tell the kids—but he texted back a thumbs-down emoji and a smiley face, the light still off in his room when we left.

want me to take notes for you? Cam turns his phone toward me, eyebrows raised in a question.

I nod. Following along with Cam's notes makes church 100% more enjoyable. The pastor's sermon is actually about Jesus, too, which makes it feel less like a random history lesson. And by the time the service ends and Cam and I file out with the rest of the congregation, I feel almost hopeful. Like maybe I could get kinda used to this.

Once we're on the lawn with the rest of the congregation, everyone falling into little conversations on the way to their cars, I try to find familiar faces in the crowd. Cam's siblings fly past in a pack of kids, his parents are talking to a young couple by the front doors, and there are a few older men who I remember checking out the latest Clive Cussler last summer.

"Skylar." Cam bumps my arm gently, and I turn to see that a whole crowd of older ladies has descended upon us, led by a very determined-looking woman. Beth. From knitting club.

She appears to be explaining something to Cam, but her soft voice is lost in the rustling of tree branches overhead and the toddler screaming from his mother's arms a few feet away. The other ladies around her nod, and although I scan each of their faces in turn, I'm never quite quick enough to read more than a word here and there.

A few of them reach to shake my hand, and I smile politely back. A headache is forming at the base of my skull with the effort of trying to piece together even a single sentence of what is going on.

At last, with more smiles and another handshake, they gather their purses and move on, and Cam and I escape to the car.

"What was that about?" I ask him once the doors are closed and we're inside.

"They wanted to tell us they signed the petition." His smile looks half like a wince. "I think they were the only ones. But a few of them did call the mayor's office to lodge a complaint."

"Every little bit helps, right?"

"In theory." Cam reaches for his watch and then grabs the steering wheel instead. "Want to go to the library? We should start boxing up…" He trails off. The last thing I want to do is pack books for the move the board has mandated. But the reality is, Cam still has a job to do. Even if this is what it's come to.

"Sure." I want to reach out and touch his wrist, but I don't.

• ● •

"We need another idea," I tell Cam as he unlocks the front door. Together, we scan the stacks we've already organized, trying to put off the inevitable moment when we have to start packing up. Anastasia's computer desk is tidy, and every time I look at it I can't help seeing her wild curly hair spilling over her shoulders, her pink-tipped fingers flying across the keyboard, bouncing in place or spinning to churn out sentence after sentence that I can't quite hear.

Cam runs a finger down his watch. He's touched it a lot, but no more taking it off and on since we last talked about it. His bruises have faded, and so has the pinched red mark that had bloomed from underneath the band. "Like what?"

I nudge his shin with my toe as we approach the front counter. "I don't know. We can think of something. What do you want to try next? We could make a few phone calls of our own to the mayor or something."

He shoots me a look.

"Okay, *you* could make phone calls. Or we could go door to door down Main Street and collect petition signatures that way?"

He looks thoughtful. "Do you think it would be enough?"

"I don't know." I leap off the counter and pace in front of him. "But we have to do something."

"What about some sort of interactive activity?" Cam reaches beneath the counter for a long-handled shelf duster and tosses one to me.

"Like what?"

He half-grins, waving his duster at me. "I haven't figured that part out yet."

We walk over to the children's section and wipe the tops of all the short shelves before grabbing step stools and heading to the tall shelves where the teen and adult books are kept.

We split up, each one of us taking a different shelf, which gives me plenty of time to think as I dust off the teen books. My mind wanders from the library to Mike and Aunt Kay (Every time I ask how she's doing, he says "good" and shrugs whenever I ask for more information. Boys.) to Cam's injured wrist. I wonder if his parents have noticed it. I wonder what they think. If they're worried he's somehow stressed about me. Do they think it's strange that Cam is in a long-distance relationship with a girl he only met last summer? Do they worry about me changing my mind about him? About God?

When Cam appears at the end of my shelf, I pretend to be very concerned about my duster, fiddling with the plastic handle.

"Do you think your parents like me?"

"Obviously." He leans against the shelf. "Wait, was that a serious question?"

I shrug like it's no big deal. "Yeah."

"Where is this coming from?"

I grab his hand as we walk back towards the front counter to put our dusters away. "Answer the question, please."

He stows both our dusters beneath the front counter. "Of course they do. What's not to like?"

I shrug. Who knows what criteria parents have for their kids' dating partners? I wait until I've got my purse in hand and Cam has the keys before I drop my next question on him. "Do you think it bothers them that my family isn't Christian?"

"Would it bother you if they did?" He runs a thumb over my knuckles as we walk to the front door, only releasing me to lock up and slide the key into his pocket.

I bump my shoulder into his as we walk to the car. "It's just…" When he unlocks the doors, I climb in and wait for him to start the engine. The fans, which are still on low from our drive in after church, whir quietly to life. "I don't think I'm very good at being a Christian. And I'm sort of afraid they'll find out."

Cam rubs his wrist absently against the steering wheel as he pulls out of the parking lot, thinking. "I don't think … … true, though. You try hard. You ask … … questions than anyone I know. You want to get it right."

I blow out a breath. Main Street whips by and changes to fields outside the windows. "Is that enough?"

"People who think they're good at being Christians are usually the ones who have the most work to do," he says. "You can't learn anything if you never ask questions. It's the people who know they aren't perfect who are usually on the right track."

I shrug, resting my head against the window. "I guess."

Cam reaches for me, threading the fingers of his right hand through mine. "Hey. When Jesus came, he didn't … … a lot of time in the church, talking to the people who had it all together. They weren't interested in him because they thought … … perfect already. He ate lunch with people who knew … … work … … do. And he accepted them anyway."

I stare at him, watch the way his left hand holds the wheel, knee bouncing gently against the side of the door. His hair is slightly too long, poking out over the tops of his ears, and I think with a pang that he must be the most perfect person I've ever seen.

If Jesus came and ate with the messed-up people, maybe it's okay that I don't have my whole life figured out, yet. Maybe it's okay if trying to love God is a little hard and complicated sometimes.

Cam's watch slips to the side when he swerves to avoid a pothole, and I think of the look on his face when I touched his bruises. Not pain. Exhaustion. Maybe Cam is just like the rest of us. Just trying desperately to make it through in the only way he knows how. Maybe he's not as perfect as he seems.

• ● •

We don't talk much the rest of the ride back to the house, both of us thinking our own private thoughts about God. At least, I thought we were until Cam says, "What about a bake sale? With the proceeds going to save the library?" and I have to mentally change the subject and point out that we don't really have anything to raise money for.

"Money isn't necessarily the problem," I point out, and he nods glumly, turning into the long driveway that leads to his house. "Don't worry, Cam. We'll think of something." The sight of Mike sitting on the porch, staring down at his phone, reminds me. "Don't forget, we've got the entire world of social media on our side, too."

Cam brightens, putting the car into park. "That's true. I forgot about that."

Mike looks up when we climb out of the car, shielding his eyes against the sun.

"How was your morning?" I stop at the bottom of the steps, letting Cam go into the house without me. "Could've come to church, you know. It might have given you some more answers to give the kids this week."

He shrugs. "Nah, I'm doing fine with you to answer my questions."

I reach to swat him, and he ducks.

"Eric didn't bother you again today, did he?" His eyebrows pull low over his eyes.

My stomach twists. "Why? Should he have? I thought it was just a flukey thing that one day." With the poster.

"It was. Definitely." He answers too fast and stands up even faster. "Want to go inside? Are you hungry?"

"Mike, wait—" Too late. He's already opening the door, calling a greeting to whoever's inside.

Grilled meat and the scent of frying onions wafts through the air, and Cam's dad turns from the stove, a flowered apron tied around his waist. He beams at us, says something about barbeque, and points to a plate of hamburgers steaming on the table.

"Mom will be down in a minute," says Cam, pulling out chairs for me and Mike. I'm seated at the head of the table, with the boys on either side of me. I'll be able to see everyone's faces from here.

Cam passes the tray of hamburgers down, and I'm so engrossed in assembling my sandwich (do hamburgers count as sandwiches?) that I don't even notice when Cam's parents join us at the table. Suddenly, as I'm reaching for the mustard, Cam's hand snags mine, and Mike extends his from the other side, his expression politely compliant.

Mealtime prayer. What else have I missed? Ears hot, I grab Mike's hand and duck my head, darting occasional glances at Cam to see when he opens his eyes. Across the table, Cam's mom speaks scarcely above a murmur, her soft voice just a breath of air to me. I guess that she's finished about four times before Cam opens his eyes, releases my hand, and gives me a wink, passing the mustard over.

Both of Cam's parents engage Mike in conversation, and Cam and I tuck into our burgers in silence, poking each other under the table before I finally put one foot on top of his. I'm just slipping into a light food coma, feeling warm and relaxed in my seat, when Mike stiffens beside me. He's bolt upright in his seat, hands out of sight beneath the table, a muscle twitching spasmodically in his jaw. Like he's trapped in whatever conversation they're in the middle of.

"What are they talking about?" I lean over to Cam to whisper this, hoping desperately that I've managed to regulate my voice appropriately.

Instead of answering, Cam leaps to his feet, whipping his napkin across the table. I follow his arm, turning my head toward Mike. A puddle of water is quickly spreading from my brother's overturned drinking glass. Mike gets to his feet, too, disappearing into the kitchen and jogging back to the table a few seconds later with paper towels in hand.

"Sorry, sorry," he says over and over, the muscles in his neck standing right out like someone has tightened them with a screw.

I lift plates and cups out of the way as the boys soak up the spill. Cam's parents throw a towel on the floor and his mom carries the burgers to the kitchen. I trail after her and pass her a clean plate as she gingerly pats down the burgers, which took the worst of the water. Dinner doesn't resume for almost ten minutes, but even after we sit down, Mike's face looks like it's been carved from rock. I can't ask Cam about it now, too worried someone will over-hear and restart whatever conversation Mike was trying to avoid.

Cam's mom leans over to ask his dad something. Mike and Cam go back to eating. I watch them all.

The lull doesn't last long. When Cam's attention jerks to the end of the table, I follow his gaze and catch the end of his dad's sentence, directed at the two of us.

"... the library?"

Now Cam has the same expression as Mike.

"It's going well." I jump in before he can answer, directing the attention away from the tension in the pinch of his lips and the way his hand has jumped to the watchband on his wrist.

Cam's dad turns to look at me. "... heard much about it. ... . you ... been up to?"

"Well," I shoot a glance to Cam, who nods at me to keep go-ing. "We're working on a petition. Trying to get people to call the board themselves. And Mike's making headway on the social me-dia, too."

His dad looks interested, putting his hamburger down to fo-cus more intently on my face. Beside me, Mike wipes his mouth and murmurs something, excusing himself from the table. I have to force myself not to watch him go. Stay focused in the current conversation.

Cam's foot nudges me under the table.

"And maybe we'll even put up some flyers," I finish, dragging my attention back to the conversation. "In some of the businesses around town. To raise awareness and hopefully get more people to sign the petition. Even though we don't know where to send it yet." I trail off before I can damage our reputation any more. Cam looks strained beside me, but his dad smiles.

"You guys ... ... doing good work. ... Have you tried ... ...?"

It's hard to hear across the table, so I lose about as many words as I catch, relying almost entirely on lip-reading. Mike is still ab-sent, and I wonder if he's upstairs or gone out, wishing I could hear his footsteps plodding overhead, or the front door slamming shut with a jangle of car keys held loosely in one hand. But I'm limited to what I can see, Cam's parents beginning to clear dishes and Cam himself looking thin and tired in the seat beside me.

"When Mike spilled"—I lean over to him—"what were your parents saying? Do you remember what they were talking about?"

"What?" The library conversation seems to have sucked the life out of him. "When?"

"Right before the water spilled." I kind of regret bringing this up. I wish I'd asked Cam something about himself, instead.

He shrugs. "I can't remember. Something about a guy who goes to our church, I think."

That doesn't make sense. Why would Mike care? "Are you sure?"

"Skylar." Cam snatches cutlery off the table, his movements snappy and quick. "I don't remember. I'm sorry."

"Okay." I grab the cups and follow him into the kitchen. "Relax. I didn't mean to bother you."

I can tell by his shoulders, the way they slump forward slightly when he loads plates into the dishwasher, that he's let out a sigh. He straightens enough to make eye contact with me. "It's okay. I'm just tired."

"You're always tired." I don't mean to be difficult. I say it like I'm stating a fact.

Cam nods. "I guess I haven't been sleeping well."

I rinse off a plate and hand it to him. "How long has this been going on?" I can't make myself look him in the eye. "Is it just since we came, or…?"

Cam puts a hand on my arm, tugging gently until I force myself to look at him. "It's not you, Skylar." He's very earnest, but there are purple shadows gashed under each eye.

"Is it just the library?"

He winces. "It's not that bad. Really." He presses my fingers to his lips, kisses them, and releases my hand again. OKAY? He flips the sign off, the pointed K letter shape definitive. The only way I can tell he's asked a question are his raised eyebrows, waiting for a response.

I nod. Communication was so much easier over text, when you either told the truth or you didn't and there was no question about it. It's so much easier to believe what you're told when it's just words on a screen, no body language getting in the way.

OKAY.

Chapter
TEN

Mike

I ALMOST THROW UP AT THE TABLE WHEN CAM'S DAD MENTIONS ALEX. I choke back the full bite of hamburger I just bit into and wipe my mouth hard with my napkin. Surely they can tell my face is going red. I must look as guilty as I feel.

I reach for the salad tongs and deliberately bump my elbow into my glass, leaping to my feet as water floods the table, most of it splashing across the plate of leftover hamburgers.

"Sorry." I force the words out, already jogging to the kitchen. Anything to get myself as far away from this conversation as I can. I take my time scanning the countertops for paper towels, picking the roll up slowly and walking back to the dining room. Giving the conversation time to fade from everyone's mind.

When I sit back down, Cam's mom clears her throat, turning to his dad. "So, did you decide what you're going to do about Alec's idea?"

Alec. My face goes hot again. Seriously? I panicked that hard and dumped water all over the table because I misheard some guy's name? I need to get a hold of myself. This is ridiculous. The $50 bill I handed through the window to Eric flashes through my mind. I started this summer with one secret, and now I have more than I can count to keep track of.

The last thing I want to do now is eat. I excuse myself as soon as I can, when the attention is on Cam and he's the one dodging questions, Skylar's lips pursed as she tries to follow the conversation.

When I get upstairs, I flop down on my bed and stare up at the ceiling. Eric won't tell anyone about Alex. And if he did, who would believe him? He's probably forgotten about it. I paid him. It's over.

● ● ●

I'm five minutes away from the end of a teaching shift next week when Eric texts again. My phone, face-up on my music stand, flashes a text preview.

We need to talk

I want to rip it off the stand right then and there, but we're just four bars away from the song we've been working on all week, and I can't ruin it now. The kids are so focused, squinting at the music and craning their necks down to peek at their fingers. Emily has her tongue stuck out, glaring at the music in concentration.

When the last chord is vibrating through the air, I set my own ukulele down and smile at them. "Okay! Good job, guys!"

Half of them dive for leftover snacks in their backpacks, or juice boxes left under their chairs, already not paying attention to me. Emily is scribbling something in the margins of her music, still frowning at the notes.

"We're just about out of time—" The half of the students not already rummaging through their backpacks for snacks immediately catapult out of their seats, ukes dangling haphazardly from one hand as they stampede toward the door.

Emily scoops up her music, sets her ukulele gently in its case, and walks slowly up to the front of the room. "Mr. Mike," she says, staring at her shoes. "I have a question."

Today, of all days? But I set my phone down and try not to look upset when I answer. "Sure. What's up?"

"I have a question about something we talked about in chapel today."

Uh-oh. I frantically try to remember what the chapel meeting thing was about today. Jesus was definitely mentioned.

"If I do something bad…" She's still staring at her shoes. "… will Jesus really forgive me?"

Ah, thank goodness. An easy one. Even I know that one Bible verse about God loving everyone. "Of course he will." If only real life was that simple.

She doesn't look convinced. "Are you sure?"

Of course not. I'd give anything for the assurance that all my mistakes would be forgotten. Instead, I ask, "Do you want to talk about what happened?" Man, she reminds me of the twins. Aiden, specifically. Sara never apologizes for anything.

Lily appears in the doorway. "Everything okay here?"

Emily peeks at her out of the corner of her eye.

"Do you want to ask Ms. Lily about what's going on?"

Lily comes into the room and sits backwards on one of the kids' chairs. "What's up?"

Emily repeats her question, and I let myself fade to the back of the room to tidy up while Lily reassures her. I'll wait until they're both gone to text Eric back.

After a few minutes, Emily bounces out the room with a cheerful, "See you tomorrow, Mr. Mike!" All order restored in her universe. Lucky. Unbidden, the social media profiles pop to mind. No matter how many posts I put up, no matter how many tweets I send, engagement is low. Follower counts are dropping as fast as they spiked. I think it's safe to say I failed my marketing class for a reason. This isn't going to happen. I should have told Skylar the truth right away. Now I've raised false hope. I could use a Jesus of my own to bail me out.

I pack my music into my backpack and help Lily set the chairs up for tomorrow's session, picking up the stands that the kids knocked over on the way out. Taking my time so I don't have to think about checking my phone.

With two of us, the whole thing takes only a few minutes. Lily heads back to the front desk to turn off the computers, and I let myself out the side door. I'll text him when I get to the car.

By the time I've got the AC blasting, all I want to do is crawl into bed and nap for a week, so I decide to let the text sit a little while longer. I drive home with some country station playing, and when I open Cam's door to the smell of blueberry muffins—there's a full plate of them on the counter, with a little note that says *please eat me*—I set my phone down, grab a muffin, and hoof it up to the peace and quiet of my borrowed bedroom.

• ● •

Only a few minutes later, someone bangs on my door.

"One sec." I haul myself off the bed, but before I can take two steps toward the door, it flies open. Skylar is silhouetted in the setting sun pouring from a window in the hall. Before I can get a word in edgewise, she marches into the room, flings my phone at my chest, and starts yelling something I can't make out, running her words together so they become just a string of letters pouring off her tongue.

"What's wrong?" I grab her upper arms and do a cursory check for blood or some other wound. "What happened?"

She brushes hair out of her face, shakes loose of my grip, and picks my phone up from where it fell onto the bed. "I PICKED UP YOUR PHONE BY ACCIDENT—"

"You're yelling at me." I try to keep the annoyance out of my tone, remember she can't hear me, and work on smoothing my expression instead. I hold my finger to my lips. Did she find the social media accounts?

Skylar's face pinches. "Don't shush me." But she does bring her voice down to a speaking level, and her fingers creep up to her throat like she's trying to feel her own voice as it leaves her body. "Someone texted you." Her glare is like lighter fluid. I have a feeling I'm the match.

That's the last time I leave my phone downstairs. "So what?" I cross my arms over my chest. Eric's name isn't saved in my phone. I'm not *that* dumb.

"I thought it was my phone, so I opened the message." She holds my phone out to me, scrolling up and down through a set of texts—Eric's, I realize, when I see the dollar sign fly by at least four times. I don't talk to anyone else about money. Not in such specific amounts. I snatch it back. "That doesn't give you the right to read them all." I slide it into my pocket, the weight a comforting reminder that she doesn't know. She's only guessing.

"Mike, what is going on?" Skylar looks like she's about to cry. "Why is Eric texting you again? Why are you giving him money? What secret does he know about you?"

Shoot. He must have texted again. I shouldn't have left my phone downstairs.

"It's fine, Sky. I promise." I meet her gaze and force the words out with as much confidence as I can muster.

Instead of going away, she sits down on the bed. "What is going on with you guys?"

I feel like sitting beside her is too much of a commitment, so I stay standing. "Nothing, I promise. Nothing like last summer."

"No drugs?"

"None."

"Parties? Drinking?" She doesn't say anything about the car I crashed last summer, but her wince, hand reaching for her hearing aid almost like a reflex, gives her away.

"Do you smell alcohol on my breath?" I scoop yesterday's shirt off the floor and toss it to her. "Weed? Anything?"

She buries her face in the shirt, sniffs loudly, and wrinkles her nose. "This should be washed."

I take it back and shove it into the laundry basket at the foot of the bed. "That's beside the point."

"Okay, Mike." She folds her arms. "But if you're not into that stuff anymore, what on earth is the money for?"

How much did he ask for this time? "It's stupid." My mouth is working ahead of my brain. I only think of an explanation at the last possible second. I should tell her the truth. But at this point, I don't know where to start. "He spotted me some cash last summer. For…you know. And now he wants it back. That's it."

She folds her arms. "That's it?"

I hesitate.

"You don't have anything else you want to tell me?"

"Trust me. Everything's okay." The words taste like ashes. Why was it so easy to tell Aunt Kay?

"You're not lying to me, right?" Skylar folds her legs under her, playing with a loose thread on the comforter.

A flash of anger surges in me. Why? She's right. "I'm not lying to you." And there it goes. The moment for telling the truth—any part of it—is clearly past.

She nods. "Okay."

"Great." I get to my feet, grab her hands, and pull her up beside me. "Stop worrying about me. Please."

The corner of her mouth twists.

"What?" I open the door, ushering her out into the hall.

"You and Cam both." Her smile looks forced. "You know I'm only worried because I love you, right?"

I pull her into a one-armed hug, although the irrational part of me feels like she'll still figure out the truth if she gets too close to me. "I know. And I appreciate it." I wonder what Cam isn't telling her. "You just worry about you, okay?"

She shrugs. "I'm okay. Nothing really going on with me." But she looks discouraged when she turns to walk down the hall, and I feel a sudden flash of misgiving. I haven't been paying attention to Cam. There's no way he can break Skylar's heart. Not now. Not after I've already done a number on her. She needs someone reliable. Open. Caring. But if Cam becomes someone she has to worry about—if he breaks up with her or puts her at risk… I can't let that happen.

"Hey," I call down the hall after her, forgetting that she won't hear me. She turns the corner and jogs down the stairs. When I walk into the living room a few minutes later, I find her curled up on the couch beside Cam, scrolling through Netflix. I cross the room and pause in the doorway to the kitchen, studying my sister's boyfriend. He fiddles with the remote, his face cast into stark lines by the lamp in the corner of the room. Has he always looked this tired?

He glances up and catches me looking, so I give him a nod and move into the other room, thinking. I thought I was the only person Skylar really worried about, and what was I going to do? I have to live with it. But my sister shouldn't have to be the strong one in all of her relationships.

I climb the stairs back to my room. How long have I held the position of "messed-up brother"? When will I stop failing her?

Eric and Alex, my failing grades and the lost internship…they all feel like weights tied around my neck. I can't help Skylar if I'm drowning myself. But I can't figure out how to get free without causing a thousand other problems, more stones around my neck, more pebbles thrown by an angry mob.

When I get back to my room, I kick the door shut, pick up my phone, and flip through Eric's texts. He wants more money to keep quiet. More money to leave Skylar alone.

I'll leave it at your house tomorrow. What else am I supposed to do?

Then I turn off my phone, flop onto the mattress, and close my eyes. Sleep evades me for a long time, and when I finally do drift off, I dream over and over that I'm dying.

First, I'm trapped, hands tied behind my back, staring down the barrel of an executioner's gun. Then, in a flash of light, as I flinch back and brace for impact, a massive constrictor coils around my body. As I'm gasping for breath, the snake vanishes from view and I'm falling through open air, hands reaching out for me and missing every time. I scream, curled into a ball, as the ground gets closer and closer—

And then with a splash, I'm underwater. At first, I'm relieved. I know how to swim. This will be a breeze. But as my clothes soak with water, my mouth dips below the surface, and I taste salt.

A fin crests the surface of the water a few feet away, and panic rockets through my veins, jacking my heartbeat up to double speed.

My head dips below the water, and no matter how hard I paddle I can't break the surface. Shadows swim around me, the light from the surface fading fast, and then the long, sleek body of a shark appears, tail flicking lazily back and forth.

Maybe he hasn't seen me.

He draws closer and closer, and I hold perfectly still, my stale breath drying in my lungs. Without warning, the shark spreads its mouth open until all I can see are teeth, and dives straight for my chest. I forget to hold my breath or swim or do anything except scream, which I do so long and loud I feel my throat tear. And as the shark rips me to pieces, pain like fire in every extremity, I scream and scream and scream.

• ● •

Someone pounds on my bedroom door, and I snap awake. Both of my arms have fallen asleep, numb and burning with pinpricks, and my sleeping bag is twisted around my torso, pulled over my face.

"Mike?" Someone cracks open the door. "Are you okay?"

I sit up and shove the sleeping bag off me. "I'm fine. Sorry."

The hall light reveals Cam standing in the doorway. "I heard screaming."

I get to my feet. "Nightmare."

We stand there looking at each other for a moment.

"What time is it?" I rub my hand against my side, trying to get the blood flowing again.

"Almost one."

"Skylar?"

"Asleep, I think. She went to bed ages ago." He's wearing pajama pants, but they're not wrinkled. Maybe he hasn't been to bed yet.

"Well." I nod, and Cam steps back. "Thanks for waking me up."

Cam shrugs. "No problem."

When he walks away, it's not back toward his bedroom at the end of the hall, but toward the living room. I pull the door closed behind him and flop back on the bed. Every time I close my eyes, I can see the shark, the water filling my lungs.

My throat feels raw. I wonder how long I was really yelling. Not for the first time, I'm thankful that Skylar can't hear. Even though it's messed up. At least she won't have this to worry about, too. Unless Cam tells her.

But somehow, I have the feeling that Cam is used to minding his own business. He might even be keeping a few secrets of his own.

Chapter
ELEVEN

Skylar

MIKE IS DEFINITELY LYING TO ME.

I set my alarm clock deliberately early—earlier than I know Mike sets his—and when the vibrating pad goes off underneath my mattress, the constant humming jarring me into the waking world, I don't linger under the covers. Instead, I haul myself out of bed, slip my hearing aids in, and reach for my sports bra and running shoes.

I make it to the kitchen in about ten minutes flat, and even though I thought I was ahead of schedule, Mike is already at the counter eating a banana.

"You're up early."

He shrugs. "Couldn't sleep. You coming with me today?"

I hold my shoes high. "Obviously. Set my alarm early and everything."

He nods. "Cool."

It's hard to tell if his lack of enthusiasm is just the early morning, or something more.

Cam's parents wander down as we're chatting, mumbling something to Mike—probably breakfast offers, which he refuses. The background noise increases significantly as they whisper to each other, opening and closing the fridge, pulling spoons out of the cutlery drawer.

Mike jerks his head toward the front door, eyebrows raised, and I follow gratefully. When the door is pulled shut behind us and all is quiet again, I continue. "No interrogations. But maybe a few answers?"

Mike leans down to lace up his shoes. When he straightens, he says, "I don't know if I need any answers from you."

"Ha ha." I reach to shove him, but he dodges me. "Very funny."

"No talking, Sky. Let's just run." There's something pleading in his gaze that makes me want to say yes to him. It also furthers my need for answers.

When Mike takes off, bouncing slightly on his toes as he jogs slowly down the long driveway, I follow. "How far are we going today?"

He turns his head so I can read his lips. "Far." He rolls his neck from side to side. "Ready?"

I'm barely warmed up, but I nod anyway. "I'll follow you."

Mike picks up the pace, and I wait a few feet behind for him to settle into his long-distance stride, giving him a few minutes to get comfortable before I catch up with him, matching him stride for stride. With Mike away at school, it's been ages since we last ran together, but we slip back into place like we never stopped.

"So—" I start, but Mike shakes his head.

"No talking, okay? Let's just run." He quickens his stride almost imperceptibly, and I'm forced to match him. This is a lot faster than I normally take my morning runs, and in only a few strides my breath is coming quicker.

Mike is already sucking in air—I can see his chest heaving. He won't be able to maintain this pace for long.

We run deep into the countryside until all we can see around us are farmers' fields and trees, like punctuation marks, at every border. There are a few tractors out, churning through the fields like ships at sea, but we don't pass a single car. And Mike doesn't slow down for ages, even though his shirt is plastered to his skin with sweat. My ponytail grows bushy in the humidity, flyaway hairs stuck to my forehead and the back of my neck, but my skin feels alive, and I can almost hear the blood pumping through my veins. It's been a while since a run was this much of a challenge.

"I love this!" I gasp to Mike, whose face is clamped down in the determined expression usually reserved for Olympic weightlifters before they hoist like a million pounds of steel over their heads. He says nothing.

At last, when I haven't had a deep breath in minutes and my right knee starts to ache, Mike slows to a jog.

"Finally," I say, hoping to start some kind of conversation.

Mike still says nothing.

"Do you want to head for home, or…?" I let the sentence trail off, resisting the urge to massage my knee. The lack of a warm-up is definitely getting to me.

"Skylar," Mike says, turning to face me, jogging backward through the gravel at the side of the road, "I really don't want you to worry about me anymore."

"Okay."

His eyebrows are pulled low, like the words are difficult to get out. Like he's concentrating hard to remember a speech he memorized at the last minute. "I just think…you worry a lot about other people. And I don't want to be one of those people."

I resist the urge to roll my eyes. *Then stop being an idiot and making bad decisions and there will be nothing for me to worry about!* But I don't say that out loud. For obvious reasons. "Mike," I start, but he's still talking.

"I'm your older brother." He slows to a walk and changes direction, heading back toward Cam's house. "From now on, I worry about you."

I don't know if this is a genuine offer or just a way to deflect my attention, but it's sweet. I sling an arm around his shoulders, leaning my head against him for just a second. "Thanks, Mike."

But it's not that easy, and I bet he knows it. I won't stop worrying about him until I know for sure he's okay with all of this—Eric, the lost internship, the social media request I just threw in his lap. Even then, I bet I'll still be trying to look out for him. You don't just forget a summer like last year. The consequences don't just vanish without a trace.

He nods, and when I pull my arm away, he steps back into a jog. "Okay?"

I match pace with him. "I'll try."

He shoots me a sharp look, but I only shrug in response. What else does he want? I won't lie to him. Even if after all this time, he's still lying to me.

• ● •

By the time we get back to the house, my knee is throbbing. I limp upstairs to shower, banging on Cam's door when I pass by. It swings open under my touch, and when I call his name, poking my head inside, I find it empty.

When I make my way downstairs again, Mike is tying his shoes by the door and the only person in the kitchen is Cam's mom, who is eating a slice of peanut butter toast at the dining room table.

"Has anyone seen Cam?"

Both of them answer at once, but Cam's mom is closer to me, so I look at her.

"He said he wanted to stop at the store on the way into the library," she says, her lips forming each word with precision. "He asked if you could ride into town with Mike."

I swing my head around to look at my brother, who nods. "He texted me."

"Okay then." I try not to feel hurt that everyone has apparently made their plans without texting me first. "Can we stop at the tattoo parlor on the way?"

Mike looks confused.

"For coffees."

His confused expression intensifies.

"I'll explain on the way." I turn to the counter, tug a Pop-Tart out of the box, and grab the lunches Cam and I packed last night out of the fridge. Cam's mom waves from the kitchen table, and I follow Mike out to the car.

By the time I've explained the tragic story of Milk and Sugar's untimely demise, we're halfway into town. Mike shakes his head, one hand resting on the top of the steering wheel as he slows the car to meet the changing speed limit.

"It's too bad." He shakes his head, glancing over at me.

"This is why the library matters so much." I clap my hands together for emphasis. "We have to fight for all the beautiful little places that make this town unique." I'm ramping up for a longer monologue, but Mike pulls the car over when we hit Main Street and instantly picks up his phone, swiping through his messages with a deep furrow line on his forehead.

"Is everything okay?" I crane my neck, but I can't read over his shoulder.

He covers the phone screen with one hand. "Yes. Absolutely. It's from, um, work."

Another lie.

"You want me to drop you off here?" He frowns up at the swinging sign that proclaims the tattoo parlor's hours. "Are you sure?"

I point to the hand-lettered coffee sign in the window. "See?"

He nods. "Maybe I'll pop by sometime."

"Want to come in now? Get a coffee for the drive?" Give me another chance to figure out what you're hiding?

He shakes his head, and when I step out of the car he pulls away as I'm waving good-bye.

When I push open the tattoo parlor door, the blonde woman behind the counter looks up and smiles at me.

"... again?" Her words are drowned out by the CD player behind her, so I wait to reply until I'm right at the counter with a great view of her face.

"Sorry." I tuck my hair behind my ear so she'll be able to see my hearing aids. "Can you repeat that?"

"Oh!" Her cheeks flush, and she tucks a strand of long, blonde hair behind her ear. "I just said, 'back again?'"

"I really liked Milk and Sugar." I scan the cookie jars, looking for chocolate chip. Today, it's peanut butter.

She nods.

"But this is nice, too," I add, afraid I've offended her. "That's not what I meant."

"I get it." She's nodding still. "It was a great place. It's hard when things change." She looks thoughtful. "Although, I shouldn't complain. The move is sort of how I ended up working here."

"Have you always been a barista?"

She turns to wipe down the counter with a damp cloth, and then looks back at me. "I've always been ... ... the food ... ... industry," she says, staring down at the counter so it's difficult to read her lips. "But bigger chains. This ... ... the first ... ... for me. And I like it." With this, she meets my eyes again, a small smile on her face. The little grey apron suits her, and she looks at home there behind the counter with a coffee cup in her hands.

I order my two coffees (black for Cam, vanilla latte for me) and at the last minute, add two peanut butter cookies to the order. "I'll be back." I waggle one coffee cup at her.

"... ... looking forward to it." She waves as I push open the door, stepping into the bright sunlight spraying across Main Street.

The library is only a few storefronts down from the tattoo parlor, so the coffees are still warm when I arrive at the door, peering through to see if Cam will notice me. I could put one of the coffees down and text him to come get me, but with my luck I'd kick the drink over before ever getting a sip. So I just dance back and forth in front of the door, hoping my shadow will attract his attention.

In just a few minutes, he appears, a grin twisting the corner of his mouth. *What are you doing?* he mouths to me, making a fist and then tapping his thumb and index finger together twice, palm facing up.

I shrug, holding up one of the coffees. "For you," I say, when he pushes the door open for me. "Black. And a peanut butter cookie."

"You're amazing." He kisses me on the forehead and reaches for the coffee, the fingertips on his right hand red and swollen. His watchband is half-unbuckled, like he was messing with it when I showed up and didn't have time to tuck the end back in.

I don't say anything, but when he catches me looking, he switches his coffee to the other hand and fixes the watchband, sliding his right hand into his pocket. "It's nothing, Skylar."

"It doesn't look like nothing to me."

He sighs, swigging back a gulp of coffee, wincing when the hot liquid hits his throat. "The skin's just irritated. Nothing ... ... worry about."

"It looks blistered." *God, I know you're not a vending machine.* I don't know how to finish the prayer when all I want to do is de-mand answers. *Can you help him? Please?*

He doesn't answer right away, taking another long sip of coffee. When he does speak, he won't quite meet my eyes. "Want to get started ... ... new poster for the front window?"

What I really want is to get some answers out of him, but since none seem forthcoming, I nod instead. "What if we did a 'share your favorite book' campaign? We could hang the poster outside and put out a tray of markers, so people could write down the titles."

"And show them ... ... invested in the future of the library." Cam nods. "Yes. That's a good idea. Then the board will have to understand why they can't just close it. They can't pretend it doesn't matter."

"I'll get the poster board." I jog over to the craft cupboard and tug down supplies, bringing them back to the counter and spread-ing paper, markers, and some of the kids' stickers out within reach.

Just as we're about to get started, Cam reaches for his pocket, a smile spreading over his face as he sets down his markers.

"Who is it?" I crane my neck, but can't see the screen.

"Ana." He cups the phone to his ear. "Hello?"

I swat at his arm. "Put her on speaker! Please?"

He obliges, but all I can hear is a crash of static. Cam makes an apologetic face and mouths, *She's in the car*. Of course she is.

"She says hi," he says, his eyes trained on the phone like that will help him translate better. "She's driving to pick Eva up from camp. She's very…excited." The pause as he tries to find the right word, and the smile that creeps over his face when he says it, makes me wonder if she's yelling into the phone in utter delight. Probably.

"… … things going … …" She comes through in a burst of clarity, just the two words. It's enough. It always feels like a victory when I can put the pieces together, no matter how small.

"Things are going okay." I lean in. And then I catch sight of Cam shaking his head.

"… … okay?" Her voice is like a squawk.

"Things are good," Cam jumps in. "Really good. We're making signs right now. We'll figure it out. Don't worry about a thing."

Overkill, much? I quirk an eyebrow at him. Surely we can be honest with Ana.

"She's asking if we need help," Cam's speaking double-quick, turning his face toward me so I can lip-read fully. "No," he says to Ana. "We've got it under control."

I glance from our empty poster board back to him. "Why? Do you have any ideas?"

Anastasia launches into a static-filled speech, and Cam does an exaggerated face palm, making a face at me. *Thanks a lot*, he mouths.

I stick my tongue out at him. "What's she saying?"

Cam still has his forehead cupped in his hand. "She wants us to do …"

"A what?"

He lifts one finger, listening to Ana. "With whose car?" he says into the phone. To me, he says that same word again, but I can't figure out what it is.

I wiggle my fingers in mid-air. FINGERSPELL?

B-O-O-K-M-O-B-I-L-E, he spells. "No," he says again into the phone. "We can't use my parents' minivan."

"How would we pay for gas?" I can't hold back a laugh at the thought of us handing books out the windows of the car Mike and I share.

Cam shrugs, flips his fingers out from his forehead in the sign for DON'T KNOW.

Ana continues.

"What's she saying now?"

I can't tell if he's holding back a laugh or a groan of despair, his eyes crinkled shut at the corners. "She wants us to go door-to-door. On foot. Carrying books."

"In what? A wagon?" I say this a little too loudly, and Cam covers the bottom of the phone where the speaker is, cocking his head like he's listening.

"She says that's a great idea." This time he can't help laughing, too. "Hey, Ana? We've got it covered. Honestly."

She squawks something else over the phone.

"No, really. We're good. We'll send you pictures of the signs." He listens for one moment more. "Okay, have fun with Eva! Bye. Bye. Yes. Bye."

At last, he hangs up the phone, and I let the giggles loose for real. "A bookmobile?"

Cam sighs into his hands, shaking his head. When he makes eye contact again, he's grinning. "Can you picture us lugging half the library around in a little red wagon? They'd never let us work here again if we started hauling dozens of books down the streets with no 'librarian' supervision." He puts *librarian* in very sarcastic finger quotes.

I reach over and give him a hug. "Want to finish the signs now?"

He reaches for a marker. "Yes. Definitely."

I make Cam do the hand-lettering, since his handwriting is better than mine, and I content myself with placing stickers at strategic positions across the board and using a ruler to draw lines for people to write their favorite titles on.

After almost an hour of painstakingly tracing and filling the giant letters that read GOLDEN SOUND PUBLIC LIBRARY FAVORITE BOOK CHALLENGE, he sets down his marker and shakes out his wrist.

"How does it look?"

I step back and cast a critical eye over the paper. "It's perfect." It will probably attract more children than adults, but maybe that can work in our favor.

Cam sighs for like the hundredth time, running a hand over his face. He covers a yawn with the back of his hand.

"Let's take a break," I offer. "Where's your coffee?"

"Gone." He picks up the empty paper cup and tosses it into the recycling bin. "I didn't sleep very well last night. I think I need a nap."

"You can sleep in the break room if you want." I rub one final sticker into place.

"No, it's okay." He stretches, hands behind his head. "I think I'll go and get some more coffee. Do you want anything?"

I shake my head. "I'm good. I'll figure out a way to hang the poster."

"Lock up behind me?" Cam waits for me to nod, then jogs down the center aisle toward the front door.

I follow him down the aisle and flip the locks behind him, waiting for him to saunter down the sidewalk until he vanishes from my view, obscured by storefronts and passersby window-shopping. Then I wander back to the counter to scrutinize the poster. If I could laminate it, it would be better protected against the rain, but then no one could fill in the blanks.

Giving up on that idea, I go hunting for duct tape or something else similarly strong enough to tack the poster securely to the library's front window. The craft cupboard proves unhelpful, and even though I pull open all the desk drawers by the front counter, I don't find anything there that can help me, either. It's not until I check Anastasia's old drawer that I find what I'm looking for. Craft supplies abound when I tug on the drawer handle.

Roll after roll of stickers, ink and stamps, brightly colored tape, and one glorious roll of extra-strength duct tape, sitting right in the middle of everything. A half-empty package of licorice nibs sits in the center of the roll, with a sticky note attached that says, *Don't eat! You can do it!*

I take the tape, leave the licorice, and carry the poster out to the front window. I'm just about to flip the locks and step outside to tape it to the glass when something moves on the other side of the door, like there's someone standing just to the right of me. I flinch—I can't help it—and spin around, holding the duct tape like it's some kind of weapon.

Eric peers through the glass, his breath making a foggy cloud on the window. When he sees me looking at him, a slow grin spreads across his face.

Open the door, he mouths, tapping on the glass.

My heart pounds. Where's my phone? I need to call Cam. Or Mike.

Eric slams his palm on the glass. Will it shatter? He hasn't tried the handle. I know Cam locked the door. Or did I? Should I run and lock myself in the staff room?

"Go away." I point away, down the street.

I want ... ... talk ... ... He points to himself, then to me.

"Go away." I point again, pulse racing. He hasn't threatened me. Cam will be back soon.

Eric says something that I'm pretty sure is a swear word, drumming on the glass with his knuckles. I inch backwards, putting a shelf between us, and then another. Eric goes back to slamming his hand against the window, but he doesn't make any move to come inside.

I peer between the books at him, crouched behind the shelf. Something catches his attention—I see his head whip around, glancing down the street—and he gives the glass one last pound with a fist and then shoves his hands into his pockets and walks away.

I let my heart rate return to normal before standing up again, walking slowly back to the front of the library to see what got his attention.

Across the street, a stream of people march steadily toward the library, and Cam and Beth, the knitting lady, are leading them. When he sees me, he waves, grinning. He must not have seen Eric at the door.

WHAT-DO? I sign to him from across the street, palms up, eyebrows down, lips pursed, because it's all I know how to do from this far away.

He grins, his hands full of our coffees, and shrugs. I'll have to get the full story from him later.

I let myself out the door and hurry to tape the poster up, glancing left and right to make sure Eric is truly gone. Then I string the tape onto my wrist like a bracelet and dust my hands off on my pants, feeling conscious and watched as the crowd draws nearer. When at last they're on my side of the street, just a few sidewalk squares away, I realize Cam is speaking to them.

"... ... need your help ... ..." He points at my poster, which I realize now is slightly crooked. "... ... Anastasia ... ..." The rest of his words are lost to the inevitable crowd noises—shuffling feet, inhales and exhalations. Someone's probably coughing in the background. Then I realize he's pointing at me.

"Hi." I wave my tape-braceleted hand. "I'm Skylar."

Cam makes some sort of concluding remark, points again to the poster, and then leans over to put his mouth next to my hearing aid. "Do we have any markers?"

"Right here." I hand them over and watch, mesmerized, as he passes them out. People huddle in groups, discuss with their friend or parent or spouse, and then, one by one, they write titles down on the sheet. A few people take selfies, and I'm kicking myself for not including a hashtag for Mike's social media profile on the sheet when a woman comes up to me, tugging a young child along by the hand.

"Excuse me," she says, "but I was wondering ... . online ... ... ?" She raises her eyebrows slightly, which is how I know she's asked a question.

Okay. I officially need those details from Mike, like, yesterday. I tell the lady to keep checking in with us and give her my email, but it's a missed opportunity.

Someone else touches my arm as the woman turns to go. I flinch—Eric?—but turn to find Beth and a few of her friends beaming at me instead.

"That was fun!" says Beth, clasping her hands together. A few of her friends chime in, but I can't keep track of who is speaking fast enough to watch their lips, so I miss almost everything. Cam is handing out markers so people can add their favorite books to the list, so I'm on my own.

"How ... ... going ... ... ?" Beth squints over my shoulder at the list of favorite books. "What a lovely idea!"

"Thanks." I wipe my hands on my thighs again, just for something to do. "It's going well. Thanks to community members like you guys."

The group dissolves into chatter again, all of them speaking over each other until I don't know who to look at next. I let myself fade into the background until Beth steps forward and says, "Will we see you in church on Sunday?"

And then I nod, half-grateful just to have understood the question. When the ladies leave, I scan the dwindling crowd for Cam and beeline straight for him.

"Hey."

He fist-bumps me and then takes my hand, watching as the last few people add their favorite books to the list and walk away. I step forward to peer down at the titles—mostly ones I've never heard of, since Mike's the reader in our family—and wait for Cam to join me.

Prince Caspian.

Peace Like A River.

Watership Down.

"How did you find all those people, anyway?" I run a finger down the list.

Dancing Through the Snow.

The Blue Castle.

The Penderwicks.

"I stopped for coffee," he says, pointing at the second line down, where someone has scrawled *The Beekeeper's Apprentice* in uneven lettering. "That's one of Ana's favorites."

"It is?" I never thought about what Ana's favorite book might be. "Wait, all of those people were in the coffee shop? Tattoo parlor?"

He grins. "No, Beth told me to poke my head in every storefront on the way back and told them about the funding problem."

Now I really wish I'd thought of the hashtag a little sooner. "You're amazing." I reach over and plant a kiss on his cheek. "Now all we have to do is get the social media info from Mike, drum up some more support, and revitalize this entire community! Call them to action!" I pump my fist in the air, kind of as a joke, but Cam winces.

I stop joking around and poke his arm. "What's up?"

He shakes his head. "Nothing. It's a great idea. Sorry." But there's this pinch between his eyebrows that says maybe he's a little stressed out. Or a lot.

"We can do this." I squeeze his hand, waiting for a smile. An agreement.

Cam nods. But he doesn't say anything out loud.

Chapter TWELVE

Mike

"MR. MIKE," SAYS EMILY, POINTING TO MY MUSIC STAND. "YOUR PHONE IS RING-ing."

I look up from correcting a student's hand position, sweat instantly slicking my palms. "It's what?"

She points. All of the other kids have stopped looking at their music and guitars and zeroed in on me and any hope of excitement. I swear, it takes twenty minutes to get them to focus and 0.2 seconds to distract them.

Sure enough, my music stand is buzzing, a blocked caller ID flashing across the screen.

"Sorry about that, everyone." I hand the guitar back to my student, lean over to my stand, and decline the call. Then I power off my phone and toss it across the room into my bag. "Where were we?"

"Is it lunchtime yet?" A little boy in the front clutches his ukulele to his chest. I'd think he was attached to it except I've seen him drop it on the floor about a million times. If anyone so much as crinkles a chip bag, he's gone.

"Not yet." I pick up my guitar. "Can everyone show me a C chord?"

Only half of them actually put their hands on the neck of the guitar. Fewer students have their fingers in the C handshape. Three of them play the chord correctly.

Across the room, my phone starts buzzing again. Everyone's head turns toward my bag. I thought I turned it off.

"Mr. Mike," says the boy in the front.

"I hear it." I wish I could just put my whole bag out in the hall. But that might raise some questions.

"Is it lunchtime *now?*" He's already set his instrument down, hands clasped hopefully in front of him.

I take a deep breath in through my nose. "I'll make you a deal." The kids perk up.

"You can eat your lunch early if you play tomorrow's chapel song once all the way through without stopping."

They droop. It's a one-minute song, but we've never made it through the whole thing in less than twenty minutes. And I'm supposed to lead them in a song during chapel this afternoon.

My phone finally stops ringing. Surely Eric will give up now.

Instead, he calls back right as the kids are about to finish the song within ten minutes—record time for this group. I tell them to go to lunch, and when they've all left the classroom, I walk out to the car and lock my phone in the glove compartment. Joke's on me if I expected it to help. I still can't get the sick feeling out of the pit of my stomach.

I only eat about half of my lunch before the bell rings for chapel and all my little students come flooding in. One of them is in tears with anxiety. Another one crosses his arms in his chair and refuses to move. With Lily's help, I manage to get the whole crew of them (minus crying child, who goes to sit with a sibling) into the auditorium and up onto the stage. While Lily announces that we'll be playing a song called "God Forgives Us" to the tune of *Baa Baa Black Sheep*, I crouch in front of the stage, flashing everyone a thumbs-up. Emily is the only one smiling. Half the other kids have their hands up to shield their eyes, staring out at friends and siblings in the audience.

"Ready?" I play a chord on my uke, hoping to draw their attention back to me. No such luck. "One, two, three, four—"

Thank goodness for Emily, who strums right along with me, singing at the top of her lungs. Most of the other kids figure out what's going on and chime in, and except for one painful moment where half of them start the wrong verse at the wrong time, we make it through unscathed.

Lily comes back up and takes the mic, and I'm shepherding the kids offstage when I hear her say my name over the speaker.

I turn to look.

"Mike? Do you want to come and tell the kids what God's forgiveness means to you?" She's waiting expectantly. Shoot. Was this part of the presentation? I know it was in my welcome package. The one I sort of pretty much skimmed, especially when they talked about chapel. Shoot shoot shoot.

I flash her my best wide-eyed *please, no*, and the girl must be a mind-reader, because she turns smoothly to the kids and says, "Okay, Mr. Mike will share with us next time! Do any of you want to share what God's forgiveness means to you?"

Hands fly into the air. I skirt the edge of the room until I'm standing right at the back, heart pounding.

The kids all give answers about God forgiving them when they get mad at their sibling, or yell at their parents. One kid says he ate his brother's brownie. And it's great that the idea of God's forgiveness can help them move on. In some ways, I'm actually kind of jealous. If only life truly was that simple.

Lily comes up to me after chapel, when parents are filtering in and kids are signing out by the door. "Sorry about that." She winces. "Didn't mean to put you on the spot. I think I got my wires crossed."

"Sorry I wasn't more prepared." I press my back to the wall and wave goodbye to Emily. "Public speaking isn't really my thing."

"I should have double-checked." She waves to one of the parents. "Hey, some of the leaders are going out for dinner when the kids are gone. Do you want to join us?"

"Thanks, but—" The refusal is half out of my mouth, just from sheer habit, when I realize I have no reason not to go. "I mean, yeah. That'd be nice."

"We're meeting at Colbie's at six." Someone waves to her from across the room. "Oop, I gotta go. Do you need directions?"

I shake my head. "Google Maps will get me there." This actually might be kind of fun. After all, no one here knows about last summer. Or school. Or Eric. To them, I'm just Mike, the music guy. Finally, an identity I can live up to.

• ● •

I wake up on Sunday morning to a text from Skylar at 9 a.m., asking if I want to come to church with them.

Got my chapel fix yesterday, I write back, since I still can't get that dang song out of my head. And then I can't go back to sleep, so I just stare at the ceiling and listen to the sound of running feet and pre-teen voices asking if the laundry's been done yet.

When the last door finally closes, I roll out of bed and grab my running shoes. I'm still wearing the sport shorts I fell asleep in last night, so I jog down the stairs, grab a banana, and bang out the front door without bothering to check if there's anyone left. I just need some space. Just need to clear my head.

I wish I could just shut my phone off and leave it in a drawer somewhere, but what if Eric bothers Skylar again? When she told me he showed up at the library, I saw red for five minutes straight. If he's going to tell her the truth about last summer anyway, I don't know why I'm bothering keeping it a secret.

I toss the banana peel into a bush and jog down the street. I'm going to tell her the truth. Just as soon as I figure out where to start. Chronologically? Should I go all the way back to last summer, explain about my grades, and finish with my social media failures? Or start small and work my way up? That, of course, begs the question, *which of my mistakes is small?* They all feel catastrophically enormous to me.

With no answers forthcoming, I give up and just run.

Straight out into the country, like the open space will allow my thoughts to evaporate. I try to clear my mind, be Zen and stuff. Think about nothing. Instead, a car drives by and I turn my head the other way, just in case it's Eric.

When a family minivan goes past, I shake my head at my own paranoia.

The run does nothing to clear my head, so I turn around and head back, forcing myself into a sprint every time I pass a country mailbox. When I reach Cam's house, I make it halfway down the driveway before I realize that I'm not ready to go back inside yet—the family could get back any minute from church, probably, and I'm not ready to face any of them yet. But I have my keys in my pocket, so I just jump in the van.

I drive as slowly as I can into town, thankful for the old shirt I'd thrown into the backseat after work on Friday, since I didn't wear one to go running this morning.

I pull the car over by the side of Main Street, in front of a pet store that's closed on Sundays, and slam the door shut behind me. It only takes a few storefronts before I realize that of course, tiny towns like Golden Sound shut down on Sunday mornings. Is everyone here Christian, or just super traditional? The bakery doesn't open until 1 p.m., and when I cross the street, I realize even the library is closed. Of course it is. I guess that's the whole point.

Just past the library, there's a tattoo parlor with an OPEN sign blinking in the window. Below it, hand-lettered on one of those chalkboard signs, is an advertisement for coffee. I remember Skylar stopping here the other day.

If there's one thing that might make me feel better, it's coffee, so I push open the door and step inside. A bell tinkles overhead, and the woman crouched behind the counter calls "just a minute" over her shoulder, frothing milk for an elderly couple peering at the artwork on the counter with concerned looks on their faces.

I scrutinize the menu items, which are taped to the front of the counter, lettered in the same gentle cursive from the window. Americano, lattes with all of the flavour shots, and something called a Highland Mist. It's a regular small-town Starbucks in here.

"What can I get you?"

I squint at the menu one more time, hoping I pronounce the name correctly. "I'll have a caramel macchiato?"

"Coming right up."

I glance up right as she's turning away again, catching a glimpse of her face in the reflection of a mirror hanging over the espresso machine. There's no way. Alex?

Her long, blonde braid swings back over one shoulder, and as she lifts a paper cup to the spout, the machine screaming to life beneath her hands, I step back from the counter. And then, because running away is what I do, I reach for the door, yank it open, and swing out onto the street.

I jog the first few storefronts self-consciously, until I'm in front of a little grocery store (which is also closed) and definitely out of sight of the coffee shop, where Alex is probably still making the drink I ordered.

I have to go back. But she'll recognize me for sure. *Aghhh.* There's no way around it—unless I pull a dine-and-dash. Without the dine. And leave her with a full cup of coffee and nothing to pay for it.

I've done enough. The least I can do now is go back and pay for my coffee. I take a deep breath, shake myself like I'm getting psyched to go onstage with my guitar, and jog back down the street, like I was trying to catch up with someone or forgot something in the van. Any sort of reason to explain why I ran from Alex.

I try not to think the word *coward.*

The bell overhead tinkles again when I enter, and Alex looks up from the register. My cup, lid and paper sleeve already on, sits on the counter beside her hand.

"You're back!" She says this cheerfully enough, punching the total into the register. I swallow hard. Does she really not recognize me? Or is she just being polite?

"Yeah, just …" I falter. "Grabbed my wallet from the car."

"No problem." She looks over at me. "It'll be $4.59. Do you want a cookie or something? For the road?"

"I'm good, thanks." She must know. My hands shake as I pass over my debit card and force myself to keep going. Keep acting like a frigging normal human being. Make conversation. "So, do you do tattoos, too?" I jerk my chin at the piece that old couple was looking at. A serpent, fangs outstretched, curls around the splintered body of a guitar. Blood—or something that looks remarkably like it—leaks from every crack in the wood.

"No, no." She laughs. "Just coffee. Trish is the only tattoo artist here, and she only works by appointment. So mostly I have the place to myself."

"Sweet." I don't know what else to say. "Thanks for the coffee."

She leans her elbows on the counter. "It's Mike, right? From McDonald's?"

Again, the urge to run hits hard. "We worked together, I think." I try to sound casual. "For a bit. Last summer."

She nods. "Thought so."

I nod, gulping my coffee just for something to do.

"You were there when I left?"

I don't know why she's continuing this conversation when I'm pretty sure we'd both like to leave. I nod.

"I didn't do it, you know." She shakes her head, mouth twisted like she's eaten something sour. "If you even remember. I'm sorry, you just came in for coffee, and I'm dumping my personal issues on you."

Except they're my personal issues, too. She just doesn't know it. "Sorry." I take a step back toward the door, hoping my body language signals an end to the conversation.

She stands up and wipes her hands on her apron. "Why? It wasn't your fault."

My throat clogs, and I cough like the coffee's gone the wrong way down my throat. "Have a good one." I reach for the door.

She nods, already turning away. "Come back anytime."

The tinkle of the bell above the door hurts my ears, the shuddering slam of the glass door shutting off the sound abruptly. The coffee stings the palm of my hand, even through the cardboard sleeve, and when I reach the car, I practically throw it into the cupholder, sloshing caramel-flecked foam across the passenger seat. *Dang.* We don't have any rags to soak up the spilled coffee, so I take my shirt off and use that instead, the cool morning air raising goose bumps across my chest.

When my shirt is half-damp with coffee stains and the seat is sort of dry, I relax back into the driver's seat and chug what's left in the cup. It has that lukewarm milky taste, but the caramel's nice.

I sit in the car with my empty cup for a few more minutes, staring out at the street. I try not to think about anything deeper than each car driving past, but with so little traffic on a Sunday morning, the distractions come few and far between.

My phone buzzes. Eric.

Hey man

I wait.

I need some money

I have my fingers on the screen, halfway through typing out *how much?* And then I just can't anymore. This has to stop. For real.

So I don't reply at all. Instead, I lock my phone in the glove box, put the car in drive, and pull a U-turn.

I'm going to Eric's house.

Chapter THIRTEEN

Skylar

CHURCH STILL FEELS WEIRD TO ME. ESPECIALLY BECAUSE I CAN'T REALLY hear the music.

I sit and stand along with everyone else, reading along with the PowerPoint slides that have the song lyrics printed across the bottom, but it feels vaguely like playing, like someone will start to giggle in the corner and we'll all laugh and admit we feel silly swaying in time to the wall of sound that relentlessly barrages my ears. It doesn't sound like music the way I remember it—in fact, it doesn't sound like much of anything at all except *noise*. Like when your neighbor decides to build a deck and turns on that super loud saw and runs it for hours and hours and hours. After a while, you forget you're listening to a saw, but it makes your ears ache anyway.

After last week's service, I looked up a few of the songs online and played them at full volume in Cam's room, earbuds tucked right against the hearing aid speakers sitting behind my ears. When I tried singing along, Cam leaned his head back on the wall and closed his eyes.

I'd stopped mid-word, caught back the next breath as the flush rose in my cheeks. "Is it that bad?" I figured I was out of tune. I didn't think Cam would care.

"No." He'd opened his eyes, blinked once or twice to see me leaning over him. "That's not it at all. I liked it."

But now, every time I think I've remembered which part we're at—once, while I'm singing at the top of my lungs—the slide changes at the wrong time. A lady sitting in front of us turns around, one eyebrow raised. Cam, his own eyes closed, doesn't see. But I want to crawl into a hole as she surveys our whole aisle, that eyebrow spiked up toward her hairline, before turning slowly forward again.

Fine. I won't sing. I'll just pray instead.

God, why haven't you figured things out with Mike yet? Oops. Too honest? *Why is there always something going wrong with him? And why don't I know how to fix it?*

Cam grabs my hand and tugs it, and when I open my eyes I realize everyone is sitting down, settling into their seats, and it's just me and my boyfriend (who has half-risen to his feet to get my attention) left standing.

I fall into that chair so hard my butt hurts when it smacks against the seat, Cam's hand still squeezing mine.

OKAY, he signs, nodding firmly. He's trying to be reassuring, and thank God he doesn't look embarrassed, but this is enough to make me renounce my conversion.

Not really. *That was a joke, God, I swear.* But I so don't want to be here anymore. You'd think the fact that I was praying would have meant I'd earn a little warning from God. But it's fine. Skylar Brady is used to being caught in situations like this.

I don't mean to sound bitter. Even if maybe I sort of am.

Cam studies me, eyebrows raised in a question. Waiting for me to tell him I'm fine.

E-M-B-A-R-R-A-S-S-E-D I fingerspell, since I don't know the sign for this word (even though I definitely should).

Cam shakes his head. CUTE, he signs, brushing two fingers down his chin and then pointing to me.

I rest my head on his shoulder, focusing on the front of the room as the pastor comes up to speak.

Don't worry about it. Cam types one-handed notes on his phone, the other arm still around my shoulders.

I pull out my phone and tilt the screen so he can see it. *Some lady turned around and made a face at me when I was singing.*

WHO? His eyebrows funnel down, scanning the pews in front of us like he's about to interrupt the whole service just to defend me.

Nvm. I shake my head. *It's just…I'm embarrassed.* I shrug.

You're awesome. He squeezes me extra hard when he finishes typing the words. *Who cares about anyone else?*

He keeps typing notes to me throughout the sermon like he did last week, writing down the Bible verse and the pastor's main points, so I get the gist of the message. But still, I can't help feeling disconnected, like everyone else has a private line to God and mine's been cut off.

Cam's phone lights up with a notification, tugging my attention back to the screen. It's an email. From an address with the word "chairman" in it.

I point frantically to the screen, and Cam opens the message. Neither one of us is paying attention to the pastor now. The email loads—it's a short one—and we lean our heads close to read it together.

Hi kids, it begins. My heart rate kicks into double-time. It's like he's replying to an email from Aiden and Sara.

Thanks for caring so much about your local library! Awesome! He's even included a smiley-face emoji. I feel like that should be reassuring, but it's awful. Silly, even.

You've worked super hard to make a difference. I know it seems hard, but the board has truly taken all the information into account in making this decision. While your little campaign is a nice idea, keeping the library running will create social ramifications that you can't un-

derstand. Keep working hard at school and trust that the adults have this one under control.

Looking forward to seeing the change you enact as conscientious adult citizens in the years to come!

He signs his name, but my vision is too blurry to read it. How could he speak to us like that? Like we've submitted a plan in crayon for him to consider?

Beside me, Cam's leg jiggles frantically as he types notes into his phone, already drafting a reply. Even when I rest my hand on his knee, it keeps right on jumping next to mine.

He switches to his messaging app and drafts a note to me. *We can't let him do this.*

I nod.

We have to keep going.

OKAY. I flash the sign in my lap and bump my shoulder into his. The chairman might have asked us to stop, but we don't have to listen.

He just likes beating on the little guy, types Cam. I'm reading over his shoulder, but he deletes the message and starts over before turning his phone back towards me. Now, the screen just reads, *I know we can do this.*

I glance over at him. He seems to be quivering, emanating some kind of nervous energy, his face sucked free of color and his eyes unusually bright. I've never been talked to this way before, but I remember Cam saying he was bullied in high school. Pushed around by jerks like Eric who wanted his notes. Jeered at and insulted for being a smart loner. I wonder if this feels like high school all over again? The tone of the email stings—and I don't even have a history with it.

I'd ask him if he's okay, except this isn't really the place for a long, in-depth conversation. So I send up a prayer instead.

Please. God hasn't answered my prayers about Mike, at least not in any way I've seen, but that doesn't mean I'm going to give up praying altogether. *Please, please, please. I don't know what to do.*

I remember that feeling of love pouring over me last summer. I know He's real. Maybe He's just...taking his time. I wait for answers, but none are forthcoming. Just the faint comfort of knowing I'm not on my own out here in the universe. God's out there, too, listening.

When everyone stands to sing the final song, I keep my eyes open and my mouth shut, watching the words flick by on the screen. After the song finishes, the pastor dismisses everyone. People burst into a thousand tiny movements as they reach for purses and stretch across aisles to shake hands and say hello.

"Ready to go?" Cam leans into me, cheeks pale. His parents are already deep in conversation with the couple next to them, and when Cam swings his car keys at them in good-bye, they wave but don't try to detain us.

"Before we go home..." I hold the rest of the thought until we make it outside, where I know I'll be able to carry on a full conversation without disruption. "Do you want to go for a walk?"

"Now?" Cam glances around us, at the farmers' fields on all sides of this country church. "We could, I guess."

"Or we could drive into town." I shrug. "I'm just...I don't want to go home just yet." The time has come. I'm going to ask him for answers. And I need some space and time and definitely full eye contact to have it.

"Town is good," he agrees, catching my hand in his. Maybe he can tell I'm about to drop a serious question on him, because he's silent as we climb into the car together. He doesn't mention the email, just turns the radio on low, shooting a questioning look at me before adjusting the volume with hands that tremble slightly.

Farmers' fields flick by the windows as we drive down the country roads, and I try to figure out how to phrase what I need to say next. How do you ask someone to reveal the very thing they don't want to talk about?

I need explanations, I could say. *Like, tell me what the heck is going on with you. Why you're falling apart over a single email.* Or I could go for something a little softer. Put my hand on his knee, look him in the eyes, and say *Hey. Are you okay? Really?*

But that feels like the question he'd just say *yes* to and move on, and I really need more than that from him today.

Cam turns the radio off, and the background noise siphons off in an abrupt curve. "We're here." He parks the car in front of the library and turns to me, putting a hand on my shoulder. "Is everything okay, Sky?"

Unbelievable. But no matter how good he is at this, I won't let him turn this around. No matter how much I'd love to let this slide and just feel his arms around me. "Everything's fine." I tug his hand down and hold it between both of mine. His skin is cold to the touch, the tips of his fingers calloused just like Mike's guitar-playing hand. Except Cam doesn't have a musical bone in his body, so I know it's from that dang watch instead. "I actually wanted to talk about you for a minute."

"Me?" He laughs, but his hand curls into a fist inside my grip.

"Yeah." I take a deep breath. How do I say this?

"You wanted to walk, right?" Cam pulls free of my grasp and pops open the driver's side door. "Let's get coffee."

I stare at him, the words half-formed and stuck in my throat as he waits. "Um, okay."

"Great." He slams the door behind him, waiting for me to get out of the car.

When I finally climb out, shutting the door behind me, Cam stretches out a hand for me. "Come on. I'll buy you a cookie."

He keeps up a steady stream of conversation, tucking my hand in the crook of his arm as we approach the front door.

"No—wait." I stop walking and grip his arm firmly, forcing him to swing around to face me. "Cam. Listen to me. Seriously."

His eyes, when he looks back at me, are pleading. "Skylar, please. I don't … … talk about this."

I cup his cheek with one hand. "I know."

We look at each other for a moment.

"Cam," I say, shaking my head when he opens his mouth to interrupt, "I need you to be honest with me."

He swallows hard, the knot of it bobbing against his collarbone.

"What's going on with you?" I spin the words as gently as possible, slow. "With the watch, the tiredness, being tense all the time, even in church. I know you're not sleeping—"

"Skylar." He does cut me off eventually. "Don't worry about me."

Everyone keeps saying that, but if they would just tell me the truth, I wouldn't have to worry half as much. I don't understand why everyone is so preoccupied with protecting me instead of talking to me.

"I do, though, Cam." We're standing on the front steps of the tattoo parlor. Inside, I can see the barista leaning on the counter, watching us through the front window. She waves at me, but I pretend I didn't see her. I don't want to distract Cam again. "So why don't you just talk to me? Please."

He sighs. "It's ... ... over the library." His eyebrows tighten, like he's just remembered something unpleasant. It rings true— the troubled look on his face heightens, like saying the words out loud hurt him a little. But it feels so inconsequential—too easy for the pain I know he's in.

"Is it?"

"Yes." He says this more firmly, eyebrows smoothing out again. "So much is riding on this. It's not just ... ... library. It's the coffeeshop closing, the board thinking people don't need community spaces ... ... because the bottom line ... ... good. Thinking ... ... can ignore ... ... for being young."

"You know it's not your job, right?" When he looks away from me, I touch his chest. "Cam? You're a university student. You have a high school diploma. You live with your parents. You know this isn't your responsibility. You have to know that."

He closes his eyes. For a minute, I think I've gotten through to him, and he'll open his eyes and drop the truth on me. But instead, he nods.

"I know."

"God's got a plan." I feel very Cam-like, telling him this. "Even if we don't know what it looks like yet." I rarely remember this, but I expected Cam to have it all down pat by now. Does everyone need a reminder sometimes? Even if they've been Christians for ages?

Cam nods along with me. "You're absolutely right. You are."

And maybe he's saying all the right things, but that exhaustion in his eyes says I haven't gotten through to him at all. This conversation has accomplished nothing.

"I know, Skylar." He looks right at me, so caring, so unwilling to let me care for him. "I'm okay. I promise."

I step into him, pulling him close to me and resting my cheek on his shoulder. "I believe you." I don't—not really—but I want to. I very badly want to.

"Do you want to get coffee now?" He pulls back so he can see my face. "Or did you want to talk more about my lack of sleep or something?" He's smiling, making light of it.

I don't know how to tell him how serious I am without turning this into some sort of Thing…so instead, I let it go. I tag along after him as he pushes open the door of the tattoo parlor, and when the barista glances questioningly across the counter at me, I order the first thing I see on the menu. Which turns out to be an Americano.

Cam gives me a strange look, like he's questioning my choices, but I pretend not to notice. It sounds exciting, Italian, like something that comes with whipped cream on top.

It turns out it's just black coffee, which explains Cam's reaction. I sip gingerly on it, trying not to wince, as Cam hands me a chocolate-chip cookie from the display, the chocolate still half-melted. Then, even though I'm drifting toward the door, Cam seems determined to linger, asking the woman on the other side of the counter how she's doing, how she likes working at the coffee shop here. I work on taking the tiniest possible sips of my coffee, not bothering to try to follow the conversation as the woman leans forward on the counter.

"Hey, Skylar." Cam's fingers brush my arm. He's all too eager to chat, as long as we're not chatting about him. "Mike ... ... right?"

"Sorry?" I tune back in, making an effort to focus. Sometimes it feels like I have to think my brain into connecting to my hearing aids. Hearing people takes a lot more work than it used to.

"Didn't Mike work ... ... McDonald's out by ... ... highway last summer?"

The woman is nodding like she knows the answer to this question.

"Sure, he did. Why?"

"We worked together," she offers, gesturing to herself. "... ... little while."

"Yeah, Mike only worked there for a few weeks."

She looks surprised. "He must have left around the same time I did, then."

"Why'd you leave?" I'm just trying to make conversation, but the way Cam's eyebrows spike and the woman winces tells me they've probably discussed this already. Or I was expected to have known it, somehow.

"I got fired," she says, her neck muscles tense. "Let go. Whatever. They thought I was stealing money, but I wasn't."

"Oh." I feel like I should apologize, but for what?

"Mike must ... ... left right after that," she continues. "We'd already been working together for almost a month when they let me ... ... Him and that other guy." She wrinkles her nose, trying to remember the name. I see her testing it on her lips. *Eric. Eric.* "Whatever ... ... was bad news. Your brother ... ... always nice to me, though."

"Mike just said he and the manager didn't get along." I feel like there's something here that should make sense to me, but it doesn't. Why didn't Mike say he knew the lady in the coffee shop? I try to remember if we ever came in together, but I'm just not sure.

"Well, thanks for the coffee." Cam waggles his cup to the barista in a quasi-salute.

I'm still thinking about Mike as the door closes behind us. Sometimes I forget he had an entire life of his own last summer. But this? I feel like this is the kind of drama he would have told me about. Especially since it sounds like Eric was probably involved.

My stomach twists. The sunlight burns the backs of my eyes as Cam jogs down the steps, turning to wait for me when he reaches the sidewalk. There's no way Mike would have gone along with something *that* stupid. Right? Even as I think the words, I remember the drinking. The drugs. The late-night driving accident that almost got so many people killed. But he wouldn't do something like this.

Eric would.

"Where is Mike working now?" Cam takes my free hand in his, looking relaxed now that our conversation is out of the way. He turns left, squeezing my fingers as we stroll down the street.

"Guitar teacher at that summer camp," I mumble. "Remember?" My heart is pounding. I need to text him. I need to talk to him NOW. I pull my hand out of Cam's and yank my phone out of my pocket.

"Skylar?" Cam stops walking. "What's wrong?"

"If you and Mike would just *talk* to me," I say, typing a one-handed text to my brother that may or may not have every single word spelled incorrectly, "maybe I could actually help you, instead of you hiding your problems from me and hurting me anyway because I can tell when you're not telling me the truth." I hit send on the text, blink back the tears that have sprung abruptly to my eyes, and try not to glare when I look back at Cam. "You don't have to take care of me! And I'm pretty sure I'd do an excellent job of taking care of you if you'd just give me a chance to try."

Cam stares at me.

"Don't pretend you don't know what I'm talking about." I toss my mostly full coffee into a nearby garbage can. "There's something going on with you. I know there is. And I don't understand why you won't just talk to me."

"Skylar." Cam reaches for me.

My phone buzzes in my hand. Mike?

"Skylar?" Cam throws out his coffee cup, too. The tired look is back in his eyes again. Maybe it never left.

It's a spam text alerting me to some deal at a store I never shop at. I don't even bother deleting the message, just slide my phone back into my pants and close my eyes for a minute.

Cam doesn't say my name again, but I can feel him there, watching me. Why do I feel like I've just added to his problems, instead of resolving them?

"Let's just go home." I open my eyes and find him looking at me, hands in his pockets. We stare at each other for a moment, and then finally he shrugs, spins slowly on one heel, and begins walking back to the car.

I keep pace with him, but his hands stay in his pockets. When we reach the car, we climb inside without speaking, the radio humming to life again when Cam puts the key in the ignition. I take my hearing aids out, cradling them in my lap, and close my eyes.

Chapter
FOURTEEN

Mike

I DRIVE TO ERIC'S BY MEMORY, TRYING TO PRETEND THAT MY PALMS AREN'T sweaty when I turn onto his street. This feels too familiar. Too much like last summer. Fifteen unread texts on my phone from Skylar. A missed call from my mom from earlier on in the week. I keep meaning to call her back, but I just…don't.

Right on cue, my phone buzzes. And then keeps buzzing, so fast and furious I think I'm getting a phone call. When I park the car and pick up the phone, though, the texts are from Skylar. Each message is jumbled and misspelled, but I think she's saying something about money. Eric. McDonald's. And…Alex? My heart rockets into my throat as I scrutinize the last message again.

> *DIF YUO SPILL MONY FOR MCDONALDS LST*
> *SIMMER WITHOUT ERIC?!?!?!??!!? I JST MEET*
> *ALECXS N HES STORYTELLER CAM*

I'd better play it safe. Not assume anything. I text her back just a series of question marks, stick my phone back into my pocket, and get out of the car. Eric's parents must be away on business again. The street is clogged with trucks and minivans parked haphazardly at the foot of every driveway. Looks like there was a party here last night. Or maybe there's one still going.

I slam the car door and walk slowly toward Eric's house at the end of the street, where the faint pulsing of a bass floats over the lawn. Someone forgot to turn the music off last night.

It feels a little like walking through the aftermath of a battle. Carnage in the form of red solo cups and empties litter the lawn. I remember what it felt like to be here for the fun part. The dancing. The heady dizziness that comes with the fourth beer in a row, chugged back heedless of taste or preference. The way girls looked at you after midnight. Brushed your arm. Walked upstairs.

And now, I feel like I'm standing outside a zoo cage, looking in. I miss the parties. But I don't miss this. The whole street reeks of hangover.

Aside from the stereo thumping half-heartedly away inside, it's like a ghost town. I can't hear anything—no one clinking dishes or making breakfast in the kitchen. No one arguing, throwing up, or still drinking, unaware that the sun has come up and a new day has begun.

I remember that, too. The forgetting. Blissful moments when nothing was wrong and Skylar hadn't been in a terrible accident and it wasn't my fault. Or it was, maybe, and I just didn't care so much anymore. When I wasn't a thief and a liar with a bad habit of hurting other people and getting away scot-free.

Sometimes, in the really bad moments, I think I'm not so upset that Skylar got hurt and Alex got fired. Sometimes I think I'm really just mad that I *didn't*.

I try to shake this thought from my head as soon as it materializes. Without the weed or the alcohol to empty my head, I have to hear myself think everything in what feels like Technicolor. Surround sound. Defined audio. Everything I've done wrong—everyone I've let down—cycling on repeat in my head. I thought I'd grown up so much since last year, but I was kidding myself. I haven't stopped failing since then.

I stand there by the foot of the driveway, considering. Eric's probably sleeping. Or hungover. I'm not going to get anywhere with him today. As I turn to go, the door flies open and Eric stumbles out. When he sees me, he points. Too late to walk away now.

Eric sways in the doorway, a white-knuckled hand gripping the frame as he stares at me. Without saying anything.

"Eric." What should I say?

"M-mm..." He hovers on the first letter of my name, like he's forgotten what it is and he's waiting for the rest to come to him. "Mike?" His tone makes it clear he's asking a question, but I'm not sure if he's asking if it's me or if Mike is really my name.

"Yep." I slide my hands in my pockets, walking slowly up the driveway towards him. Eric pulls the door half-closed behind him and slings himself into a sitting position on the front steps. His hands tremble, and he clasps them together, lets go, rubs his thighs, then scratches the back of his neck in jerky, twitchy movements, craning his neck to keep me in sight.

"What you doin' here, man?" He leans against the side of the house, purses his lips like he's taking a pull, sighs. Stands up straight. Leans over again. Scratches his arms until I see raised red welts appear on his pale skin. "Have you been here the whole night?"

"Just got here."

Still scratching like the fabric from his clothes is agonizing against his skin, he doesn't seem to notice me looking. His eyes, too, won't stay still—darting around in his face like he's looking at twenty of me and trying to take a head count.

"'m glad to see you, man. Missed crazy party last night."

"Doesn't seem like I missed much." Inside, someone's passed out—or died—right there in the entryway. Eric would have had to step over their body to get to the door.

"Did you meet the new guy?" Eric doesn't wait for a response, his eyes lighting up like it's Christmas morning. "Try the new stuff?"

"What are you on?" I don't know why I'm asking. I don't care.

"The good stuff, man, the good stuff." He repeats this phrase a few more times under his breath, shifting his weight eagerly from foot to foot. "It's so good. So good." Eric's head wags back and forth, once. Twice. Three times rapidly. He sighs again. "I can't feel anything at all. I can't remember anything." He barks out a laugh. "What did you say your name was? Did you try this stuff? Did you like it?"

I don't say anything, but he nods like he's heard the answer he was looking for.

"Right on, man. It's so good. That's right."

I nod.

He keeps on talking. "Come on in, man. Grab a beer. I'll find him." He mumbles to himself for a moment, flopping down to a seated position on the steps. "Chris! I'll find Chris and get him to front me the cash for another hit." His eyes sharpen on me. "Next time, you buy your own. And you owe me."

"I'm not giving you any more money." I square my shoulders and stare him down. He will not change my mind. This is over.

Eric's whole body seems to snap to attention, and I'm reminded of our conversation in the parking lot. How he seems to dance between high and sober at his own leisure. "What?"

"You heard me. I'm out."

Eric grins, surprising me. "What about your precious sister?"

I say nothing.

"Skylar?"

How can he remember her name when he's this high?

"I'll tell her about the money you stole." He's playing, thinking he's got me like a cat and mouse.

"What about what you did?" I step forward, looking down on him sitting on the steps. "What about what you did to Alex?"

I expect him to retaliate, trying to pull him into some sort of fight so we can just end this. Declare a winner and walk away. Last summer, I let him needle me, let Skylar walk away and just took the brunt of his words without fighting back. Now I'm out for blood.

"Alex?" Eric looks genuinely confused. "Whatever, man. That was nothing." He leans his head against the bricked wall of the house, grinning lazily up at me. "But your sister—"

"I'm going to tell her about Alex." I lean down. "So your bribery and manipulation won't get you anywhere anymore."

"Yeah, yeah." Eric seems unbothered. "Alex, right. Great guy." He trails off, mumbling something to himself, scratching the back of his hand absently, over and over and over again. More red welts appear. I wait for lucid, sober-seeming Eric to return, but instead, he gets to his feet, wanders onto the lawn, still talking to himself, counting something on his fingers.

I watch him for a few minutes, but when he turns around, he sits down on the steps again without acknowledging me. He's still talking to himself, eyes closed, something about winning an argument with someone whose name I don't recognize.

"You're not really in control of anything, are you?" I can't stop staring at him, wondering how I never noticed that Eric was more like a shell than a real person. Just an image. An illusion.

"Nope." He opens his eyes and looks right at me, but I don't think he knows who I am. "Never have been. Figured that out pretty quick." He pounds his fist against the wall until his skin is scraped raw and a thin trickle of blood runs down his wrist.

His face is blank, expressionless, and he folds his hands in his lap without looking down to inspect the damage. I want to walk away. Get in my car. Pretend I never saw this side of him. But he keeps speaking, and I'm held in place. Curiosity? Morbid satisfaction? Basic concern for his well-being? I don't know what it is. But here I am.

He wasn't like this last summer. Was he? The Eric I remember was formidable. Cocky. Authoritative. This Eric looks more like the homeless people who lurch across the street near the university, their walk ragged and their faces worn from screaming at invisible demons.

"This." He gestures to himself with his injured hand. "This is all I have. This is what I'm in charge of. I take care of business. I take care of it all. Look at me, huh?" He gestures to himself again, repeating the motion, a constant jab of his thumb toward his chest. "I'm good. I'm good. I found a solution that works. Get it? It works. I'm good."

"Okay. I get it." I take my keys out and hold them in my hand, jingling them a bit so they clink against each other. Trying to give myself a cue to leave. "I'm going to go."

"I'm good," he tells me again, still gesturing to himself. His head drops forward into his hands. "I'm all good."

I leave while he's not looking at me, my skin crawling. What's next for him? Where does a guy like Eric go except down? Will he remember me the next time he sees me? Will his parents kick him out when they return next week, next month, next year? Or will he be sleeping off a high? Will they tug his bedroom door closed, tell themselves he'll figure it out, and leave him to medicate himself into an early grave?

I had someone to throw me a lifeline. Haul me back from the edge. And if I could find a way to shift the guilt once and for all, the whole rest of my life is waiting for me. When I glance back, Eric trips and nearly falls down the concrete steps. What a mess.

When I reach the car, I slide into the driver's seat and lock the doors behind me, resting my forearms on the steering wheel as I stare across the street at Eric's house. He reaches clumsily into his pocket, hands shaking, and pulls out a joint, which he lights after three tries, huffing a cloud of smoke into the air. I was so well-acquainted with my own demons, it never occurred to me to wonder who or what was chasing Eric. Now I'm the guy with the answers. The one who got away. I could flip it on him and tell the whole town about his role in all of this. Ruin what little security he has left. Make sure he ended up with a record. The power of the next move—of *my* next move—hangs in the balance.

Someone emerges from the house, stumbles down the steps beside Eric, and throws up in the front garden, hands braced against their knees. Eric doesn't look at them, and after a moment, they go back inside, slamming the door shut behind them.

I bet he won't remember any of this tomorrow.

For the first time, I wonder what else he's trying to forget.

• ● •

I sit like that for a few minutes longer, staring blankly out the front windshield. When I check my phone, I have one more text from Skylar in response to my question marks.

I want to talk to you

I lean my forehead against the steering wheel for a second before replying. *Me, too.* Just not yet. *I'll be home later. Going to Aunt K's*

It takes less than ten minutes to get to my aunt's place from Eric's house, and I don't have any new texts from Skylar when I get there. I turn my phone to silent and slide it into the pocket of my jeans before getting out of the car. The yard is quiet—no Aunt Kay on the porch today—so I walk all the way up to the front door, although I hesitate before knocking. I feel like she'd want me to walk in. I used to, last summer. But it feels too much like an invasion of privacy, so I rap my knuckles on the door and step back, waiting.

My aunt answers the door just a few minutes later, a brightly-colored long dress whirling around her ankles. "Micah!"

"Hey." I shove my hands in my pockets. "I figured I'd check in and see how things were going."

"You are always welcome here." She pulls the door wider for me, and I follow her into the kitchen. "What brings you to my side of town?" She turns before I can answer, gesturing to a seat at the kitchen table. "I know it's not just to check up on me, so don't even try to sell me that one."

I flop into the seat and rest my elbows on the table. She sits down across from me. "You're right."

"Aha!" She raps the table, grinning. "You look just like your dad when something's on your mind."

I wince at the thought of my parents.

"Still haven't told them?"

Man, she doesn't miss much. "Nope."

I'm expecting a lecture, but she just nods. Like she's waiting for me to say more.

"I did something hard." I don't want to get into the details about Eric with her. I definitely don't have time to unpack that part of the story. "And I expected to feel better afterwards, but I don't."

Her face softens, and she leans forward slightly. But she stays quiet.

"I don't know." I shake my head. "It's like…doing the wrong thing creates such a huge—" I dodge the swear word, catching it just in time— "mess. But doing the right thing isn't any easier."

Aunt Kay shakes her head. "No, it certainly isn't."

"And I just feel…" I can't finish the sentence. I don't know how.

"How do you feel, Micah?" Her words are very soft.

I shake my head. Lost. Tired. Lonely. But I don't want to say those words out loud. "I feel like I wish it was simpler." As simple as the words *God forgives us*, sung to the tune of an old children's rhyme. "The kids I work with, at camp, they think everything can be fixed with a wish and a prayer. I guess I just wish it really was that simple."

Aunt Kay smiles. "You know, things rarely are. That simple. Even for praying people."

My laugh sounds like more of a bark. "I knew it sounded too good to be true."

My aunt shrugs. "You'll never know unless you try."

I know she sees the sudden expression of confusion on my face, because she laughs when she looks over at me.

"All I'm saying is, I've been a lot of places. Met a lot of people. And I've never found anyone who had a particularly simple life." She clears her throat, twisting a silver ring around her thumb. "But I have found more than one thing I couldn't explain. More than one person who believed in something I didn't understand." She's staring down at her hands like she's seeing something else. "It makes you think. Makes you wonder, that's all." She tears her gaze back to me. "Sorry. Memory lane."

I shrug. I don't really know what to say.

"I just mean that you shouldn't knock something for being too simple. Not without exploring it first."

"Exploring it?"

"Sure." She traces a shape on the table with her pointer finger. "Like you'd consider anything else. Do some research. Ask some questions. Then make your decision."

I tilt my head, watching her trace more shapes. I'd never thought of it that way before.

"What do you want, Mike?" Her hands still as she looks over at me.

I want it to be real. Skylar's hope. The kids' blind faith. I shake my head. "I don't know."

My aunt watches me for a moment, then claps her palms down on the table and stands up. "Will you stay for lunch?" She glances down at her watch. "Or early supper?"

Visions of firefighters fill my mind, replacing all other thoughts. Grateful for the distraction, I stand, too. "Only if you let me cook."

Chapter
FIFTEEN

Skylar

I'M TRYING TO CONVINCE MYSELF TO GET OUT OF BED A FEW MORNINGS later, scrolling aimlessly through Instagram, when Mike texts me.

You up?

Yep!

He appears in the doorway a few minutes later, dressed in khaki shorts and a camp tee shift. If he's leaving for work already, I've overslept.

He says something to me, lips moving, but I don't have my hearing aids in yet. Whoops.

"One sec." I hold up a finger and hook the coil over my ear with the other. I'm so much better at this than I used to be. "Okay, sorry. What?"

"Aunt Kay wants us to come for dinner tonight." He waggles his phone at me. "Are you and Cam free?"

"Definitely!" I throw the covers back and sit up, hunting for a clean shirt. I really need to come up with a better system here.

Mike surveys my clothes-covered floor with disdain. *His* shirts are all neatly hung up and organized by color. But who has time for that? "Okay. I have to go to work. I'll tell her you're available."

"Wait, Mike."

He stops, one foot already in the hall. "What's up?"

"How's it going?" When Mike winces, I clarify, "At camp?" I have to find a good time to ask him about the girl at the coffee shop. But not now. After the stream of texts I sent him the other day—and the explanation he refused to give, no matter how hard I tried to corner him—we haven't talked much. Mike's been going out in the evenings with some of the other counsellors. He comes home smelling like coffee or fries—never beer. Never weed. Maybe he's asking them all his questions now.

"It's good." He jerks a thumb towards the door. "I gotta go, sorry. See you tonight."

He closes the door before I can say anything else. It's good that he's going out with his co-counsellors. I just wish I knew what was going through his head! Is God starting to get through to him, even if I can't see it?

At last, I find a pair of shorts and a shirt that work together, and I grab a hoodie of Cam's that I stole to wear to bed and shrug it on over top. It'll be hot later, but Cam's parents have the AC set low.

When I step into the kitchen, rolling up the sleeves on Cam's hoodie, his mom is sitting at the counter, drinking coffee.

"Good morning." She sets down her mug instead of mumbling the words into her coffee like most people do. "Feel free to help yourself to breakfast. I didn't have time to bake anything fancy today." She winces in apology.

"Morning." I cover a yawn. "I think I'll make toast, if that's okay."

"Enjoy!" She tips her coffee to me in salute. "Do you know where to find the toaster?"

I flash her a thumbs-up, pulling it out of the cupboard and plugging it in before dropping two slices of bread inside. I pull the peanut butter and jam from the fridge and line them up on the counter, leaning back against it while I wait for my toast to finish.

Cam's mom sips her coffee, scrolling through her phone before glancing back up at me. "It's going to be a beautiful day, I think. Do you and Cam have plans?"

I nod. "Back to the library, I think."

She nods. Cam's mom has a great face for lip-reading—warm and expressive, words perfectly enunciated every time. "How's that going, by the way?"

I shrug. "No one will reply to our emails. But we're doing our best. Beth, from church, is helping too."

"Oh, yes." She grins. "They're quite excited about it. She was telling me the other day that they've been calling the board members every morning to complain."

"Really?" I didn't know. I bet Cam didn't, either. I turn to check on my toast and it pops up right before my eyes. What else is happening behind the scenes? First we've got Mike's social media campaign, and now this. Yes!

When my toast is sufficiently slathered, I carry it over to the island and slide into the chair next to Cam's mom, folding my hands and ducking my head in a self-conscious prayer.

We sit in silence as I polish off one slice. Shoot. I didn't even think of asking her about *her* day. I pause before biting into my second slice. "What about you?"

She glances up from her phone. "Sorry?"

"Do you have any plans for the day?"

She smiles. "I have to drop the kids off at camp in an hour or so. I think it's the same one where your brother's working, actually."

We make small talk about the camp for a few minutes, and then the conversation lags again. I finish off my toast. Is it rude to walk away? Or is our conversation considered over if we haven't spoken in thirty seconds?

Cam's mom saves me from making the decision by asking another question. "How are you and Cam doing, Skylar?"

"Um..." Why is she asking? Is something wrong? "Good. I mean, really well. I think. Thank you."

She laughs. "It's okay." She, like Cam, makes the O handshape and then slips her fingers into a K, thumb dividing her out-stretched pointer and middle finger. "I didn't mean to scare you. I'm just…being a mom. Checking in. You know. Cam takes this stuff so personally. He's got that small-town spirit at heart."

I wonder if she's thinking of the high school bullies, too. The personal experience that gave Cam the passion for sticking up for the little guy. "Yeah, I think we're doing really well." I pause. I don't know what to say. I don't know how much he tells his mom.

"I'm glad to hear that. I—" And then she glances up, eyes going to the stairs, and a few seconds later, Cam himself bursts through the doorway and into the kitchen, grinning when he sees me with the peanut butter.

"Hi, Sky. Hi, Mom. Peanut butter sandwich?" This is to me.

"Want me to make you one?" I waggle my empty plate at him. "Oh, also, Aunt Kay wants us to go for dinner tonight."

"Excellent." He leans forward like he wants to kiss my cheek, then hesitates, thumping me on the back instead. "She's back on her feet?" He's blushing.

I nod.

Cam's mom stands. "I'll leave you guys to it." She wanders off into the living room and Cam puts an arm around me, leaning his head against mine.

"… … up?" He pulls back so I can read his lips. "Sorry. What's up?"

"Nothing much. Mike left for work already. Breakfast with your mom." I shrug. "It's been a chill morning so far."

"Oh, speaking of Mike—" Cam steps back and snaps his fingers. "We have to get that social media login from him. I really want to see the page."

"Me, too." I pull out my phone. "I'll text him right now. Maybe he can send it over lunch break."

"Is he coming to dinner tonight, too?"

I nod, typing. *Hey. Can you send the social media login??*

"I hope she makes lasagne again." He says this with such a

devilish grin that I know there's more to the story. He's practically begging me to ask.

"Why?" I quirk an eyebrow at him.

He grins. "We went for dinner last fall, and she forgot to put the oven on while she was making it, but instead of just ordering pizza or something, she insisted the noodles were supposed to be crunchy and served it anyway."

I hold back a choked gasp.

"Oh yeah." He nods. "The crunching was so loud no one could talk, and the sauce was cold, and the cheese wasn't melted at all."

I wince.

"It was terrible," he says, but he's smiling.

"Should we pack snacks?"

Cam's still grinning. *This* is the boy I fell in love with. This is the Cam I remember. I squeeze his hand.

He nods his head, probably still thinking of my aunt. "Definitely."

Chapter
SIXTEEN

Mike

"ARE YOU COMING OUT TONIGHT?" LILY STACKS ONE LAST FOLDING CHAIR AND blows a stray hair out of her face. "Some of the counsellors are doing a little road trip into the 'big city' tonight." She puts air quotes around the words, her eyes practically disappearing into her well-used smile wrinkles.

"Nah." I tug the collar of my shirt. It's a warm one. "Family dinner. Thanks for the invite, though."

"No prob." She waits for me to grab my backpack and then follows me down the hall, calling to one of the other counsellors about their carpool plans. "You're going to family dinner, we're going to family dinner—" she slings an arm over another counsellor's shoulders. I can't remember her name, but she does a lot of talking from the front. "Same same."

"Next time?" I ask, pulling my car keys out of my backpack.

"Definitely." Both girls wave, heading off to the opposite end of the parking lot.

I unlock the car and shoot Aunt Kay a text to let her know I'm on my way. *Don't start cooking without me!*

I should know better than to think she'd listen. When I let myself in a few minutes later, the house has a very distinct smell—of smoke. Not of food.

"Oh, Micah!" Aunt Kay pops her head out of the kitchen as I slide my shoes off at the door. "We're having spaghetti tonight," she says, leading the way into the kitchen, where smoke is definitely rolling out of the cast-iron skillet. She has the heat on max and whatever used to be in the pan (onions?) is totally burned now.

"Can you open a window for me?" I reach for the dish towel and begin flapping it under the fire alarm, just in case. "I'm kind of, um, warm in here."

"Oh, don't worry about the alarm." Aunt Kay opens the window anyway. "I took the batteries out after it kept going off."

I grit my teeth. *That's kind of what it's for.* I carry the skillet to the sink and scrape the burned bits off.

"Have you told your family about school yet?" Aunt Kay leans her hip on the counter beside me. Straight to the point, as always.

I wince. "Not yet. I want to. But I can't find the right moment. Skylar is so busy with the library. It never seems like a good time."

She squeezes my shoulder. "Sometimes, there isn't ever a good time for bad news. You just have to—" In the living room, the FaceTime incoming call sound chimes. "Oh, that must be your family!" Aunt Kay claps her hands. "They're early! I'm going to go answer that call. I'll be right back!"

I fry another batch of onions and beef quietly at the stove by myself, dumping the jar of tomato sauce on top when the meat browns. The doorbell rings after another minute or two, but before I can even step in that direction, I hear Aunt Kay calling, "I'm coming!"

She opens the door and ushers Cam and Skylar into the entryway, the iPad chatter from our family back home creating a wall of white background noise.

"Mike!" Skylar carts the iPad into the kitchen, our family spread out across the screen. Aiden and Sara wave enthusiastically at the sight of me. "Come say hi!"

"Hi, everyone." I wave a spatula at the twins.

"Mike, how are you?" It's Mom's voice, but I duck out of frame and let Skylar talk over her, quizzing the twins about their summer activities. She keeps looking to Cam to repeat what's said on the video, and it ends up being a lot of voices when Aunt Kay jumps in and starts talking about her recovery after her trip.

Finally, when the spaghetti noodles are soft and the parmesan is grated, Aunt Kay ends the video call and orders us all to sit at the table so she can serve. She heaps each one of our plates with a generous helping of spaghetti and settles herself in her seat, sighing heavily.

"I've missed you all so very much." She twirls some pasta around her fork.

"I'm glad you're feeling better." Skylar beams at her, cutting her pasta into tiny, bite-sized pieces like she always does. "Tell me everything about your last trip!"

Am I imagining it, or is our aunt winking at me? "Oh, I will. But first I want to hear all about you. Does anyone have any fun stories to tell? Micah?"

Why is she singling me out?

"I'm good." I lift a huge forkful of spaghetti to my mouth to end all further attempts at conversation. She's not, is she? I'm overreacting.

In my pocket, my phone buzzes. It's probably the camp group chat. I know Aunt Kay is happy to have everyone together, but if I'd known she was going to try to not-so-subtly nudge me into a sharing session, I would have gone out with them, instead.

I mean, I wouldn't have. Not with her this excited about it. But at this very moment, I wish I was there.

Luckily for me, she seems to have shifted her attention to Cam and Skylar. "So, you two," she says, winding spaghetti around her fork. "How long have you been dating?"

She definitely knows the answer to this question already, but I'm so glad to be out of the spotlight I don't call her on it.

Skylar blushes. "About a year. Since last summer."

Aunt Kay's smiling too. How did I end up spending so much time with such ridiculously happy people?

She asks them all the normal questions about their relationship, and they seem just thrilled to answer, grinning at each other in that sickeningly in-love way new couples have. I help myself to another serving of spaghetti and go on eating.

I don't really start paying attention again, preoccupied with my own problems, until I notice Cam shifting awkwardly in his seat.

Aunt Kay clears her throat. "I heard all about it closing, you know. Terrible business."

She must be talking about the library.

Skylar grabs Cam's hand and squeezes it. She's not looking at Aunt Kay, so she probably didn't hear what she said. But she's picking up on Cam's body language, just like I am.

Okay? I see her mouth to him, and he nods.

"We're doing our best to save the library," he says out loud, adding extra detail probably for Skylar's benefit.

"Oh," she says, her head whipping around to look at our aunt. "That. We've got a plan." Her hand is still protectively covering Cam's. "I mean, yes, the chairman of the board we're fighting is a total jerk, and the church ladies said their calls are going mostly to voicemail, but Cam's full of good ideas."

Cam winces.

"He's doing a really great job. And Mike's got that social media platform going."

Everyone turns to look at me.

"He does?" Aunt Kay raises an eyebrow at me.

I didn't really want an audience for this conversation.

Cam leans forward. "About that, actually. I wanted to ask how many people you think your platforms are reaching? A thousand? Less than that? More?"

I expected to tell Skylar alone. Low-stakes. Minimal damage control.

Everyone stares at me.

"Okay, um." Should I say it fast? Just get it over with? "I haven't been totally honest with you."

Skylar freezes in place, her mouth slightly open. If I could read her mind, I'd guess she's thinking *I knew it*. Or maybe, *How bad is it?*

"I created pages for everything but...they've kind of...not worked."

Cam flops back in his chair, running a hand over his face. "They didn't?"

"What?" Skylar's face flushes all the way down her neck. "Mike?"

Cam's skin, on the other hand, is blanching.

I stare at the table. "I failed out of first year business. That's why I didn't get the internship. One of my lowest marks was marketing. I don't know much more about it than you do. I tried. I promise I did. But it just didn't take off."

There is absolute silence. A clock ticks. I never realized there was a clock in this room before.

"Well," says Aunt Kay, when it becomes clear that no one else is going to carry the conversation forward, "Does anyone want dessert?"

Cam stands and excuses himself as Aunt Kay describes the different dessert options, and Skylar is so busy staring after him that she misses Aunt Kay's spiel and has to have the whole thing repeated.

When he comes back to the table a few minutes later, looking paler—I didn't think his skin could actually *get* any whiter, but I guess I was wrong—I start stacking plates, passing them down to him.

"Maybe we'd better go," I suggest, when no one answers the dessert question.

Aunt Kay rises. "Do you kids want brownies for the road?"

Skylar winces. It takes me a minute to remember the firefighter incident from last year. My sister hasn't touched a brownie since. "Not for me. Cam?" She's still bright red. She won't meet my gaze. "I'll get the plates." Cam scoops up the whole stack and vanishes into the kitchen. Skylar watches him go—then, turns to shoot a glare at me.

I know I deserve it.

Chapter
SEVENTEEN
Skylar

WHEN I WAKE UP THE NEXT MORNING, ALL I CAN SEE IS CAM'S FACE WHEN Mike said there wasn't any social media worth speaking of. The way he beelined for the bathroom and came back breathing hard. The solid lines of his face in the car the whole way home, the absent kiss he brushed across my forehead before disappearing into his room. And the light that was still on when I woke up for a glass of water in the middle of the night.

I give myself a shake and reach to pick up my phone. There are four unread messages from Cam.

> *Can Mike drive you to library today?*
> *Thought of something, couldn't sleep. I wanted to go in early and put a few plans together*
> *I just realized maybe you would have wanted me to wake you up*
> *Sorry*

It's the last text that kind of gets to me, the apology. It feels so…defeated, somehow. So unlike Cam.

Still, I have trouble assuming everything's fine.

It's 7 a.m., I text back, squinting at the clock. Cam's texts came in a few hours ago. *Are you there already?*

I wait a few minutes for a reply, but when I don't get one, I message Mike instead and ask for a ride.

I'm leaving at 8, he texts back. *I can take you.*

Even after I shower and change, my breakfast Pop-Tart stowed in my backpack, it's still only 7:30. And Cam's still not responding to me.

"Mike?" I rap my knuckles on his door, forehead pressed to the wood. "Any chance you want to leave a little early?"

He pulls the door open, causing me to stumble forward a few steps. "I don't even …… … if the camp will be open …… … early. Is it important?"

"Please?" I fiddle with the strap of my purse. "Cam's been at the library for hours already, and I'm kinda worried about him."

Mike studies me. "He's at the library? This early in the morning?"

I feel disloyal for telling him I'm worried, but he's right. This is weird. Cam is being so weird. And he's not texting me back.

Mike studies me. "Yeah, I'll take you." He grabs his backpack off the floor and slings it over one shoulder. He looks like he wants to say something else but just shakes his head, his gaze floating to the floor.

I swallow past the lump in my throat. "Why didn't you tell us earlier? We could have helped you. You could have told me about school before we even got here. I wouldn't have—" I'm going to say I wouldn't have gotten us into this mess by asking him to help, but I think the better of it.

"It's not that easy." Mike stops to fill his water bottle at the sink. "I'll meet you out there, okay?"

"Okay." I let myself out the front door and use my set of keys to unlock the car, sliding into the passenger side, since Mike's dropping me off.

Mike comes out just a few minutes later, closing the door gently behind him. Oops—I didn't even think about whether Cam's family was still sleeping. Mike would have told me if I was speaking too loudly...I think. I hope.

Mike flops into the driver's seat and puts the key in the ignition, flipping the fans on low and turning the radio off before turning to look over my shoulder as he reverses down the driveway. "So why did your boyfriend say he needed to be at the library at, like, 5 a.m.?"

He's changing the subject. For now, I let him. "I'm not sure." I twist the strap of my purse in my lap. "I knew he was stressed about the library, but this is different. The look on his face when you..." I clear my throat. "Last night. I'm worried about him."

Mike pulls onto the main road and eases immediately onto the gas. "You don't think he'd do ... ... stupid, do you?"

"No." My answer comes almost before he's finished the question. I know it's too quick. I know I sound defensive. "Stupid like what?"

Mike shakes his head. "I don't know. I'm sure it's fine."

"He'd tell me if it wasn't." But would he? Clearly Mike didn't feel the need to confide in me about anything going on in his life. And I still don't know what's going on with him. At all.

"Mike, do you—"

"I want to tell you some stuff, Sky." Mike interrupts me. "But not right now. When you're rushing to meet Cam."

I chew on the corner of my lip as the fields flick past. Is there any way we could at least start the conversation? But Mike's right. If we start, there's no way we'll stop when we reach the library. My stomach aches. There are so many lies to unravel.

• ● •

"Thanks for the ride," I tell Mike when we reach the library, opening the door and pausing with one foot still in the car. "Hey, I still want to talk to you. About school and stuff." I pause. When I say it all out loud like that…it's a lot. "I want to know it all, Mike. No more secrets." If I'd pushed him for answers sooner, maybe this could have been avoided.

"We'll talk later." Mike leans an elbow on the window. "I promise, Sky. We will. Just go in there and find Cam."

"Okay." I step away from the curb and wave when Mike pulls away, jogging the few steps up the sidewalk to the library.

When I try the door, it's locked.

I'm here, I text Cam. I have a key, but it's buried deep in one of the pockets in my purse, and I don't feel like upending everything in my bag in order to find it.

He doesn't text back, so I lean in close to the window and look for him, squinting down every shelf until I run out of room. The lights aren't even on in there. My heart rate kicks up a notch. Where is he—what has gone wrong? Did he have an accident on the drive in? No, we would have passed his car on our way by.

This is a small comfort: there are still a thousand other places he could be. But I'm most concerned with why he isn't *here,* where he said he'd be.

I'm so busy peering in through the glass that I don't realize I'm not alone until someone touches my arm.

I leap backward, swinging my purse in front of me like a shield. I haven't been caught off-guard in a long time, always scanning my surroundings so I can make sure that this exact scenario never happens. When my eyes focus on the person who startled me, he's *laughing*…so it takes me a minute to recognize his face.

It's Eric.

No, no, no. My heartbeat kicks up *another* notch, and I wish deeply that I was with Cam or Mike, or I had the library key in my hand or a nice solid pane of glass between us. I can't stop thinking about the creepy texts he sent Mike. Remembering his face as he peered through the glass a few weeks ago. He wouldn't hurt me, would he? This is Golden Sound, and it's early in the morning on a weekday, no less. Maybe if I don't say anything, he'll go away and leave me alone.

"Hey, Skylar." Eric leans against the wall beside me.

No such luck, I guess. "Eric." I rummage deep in my purse, trying to find my key. I wish I was more organized. Mike would have his on a keychain. Anastasia would have hers on a lanyard around her neck, probably. But no—Skylar Brady has a purse full of junk, no library key in sight. I can't even pin the keys between my fingers in self-defence.

"... ... Mike recently ... ..." Eric leans in, so I catch part of the sentence. I'm not really interested in hearing the rest.

"Sorry." I continue digging through my purse. "I'm a little busy right now. Can we talk about this later?" Or never.

He touches my arm again—nothing crazy, just a tap—but I reel back. Out of reach. I need to get inside the library. Where is Cam?

"Please don't touch me."

He shrugs, lifts his hands in surrender. "Sure. Whatever. No need to be so sensitive." He swears—or at least I think he's swearing, judging by the facial expression and lip shapes. I'm not putting my best effort forward at the lip-reading right now.

Please, please, please let me find this key.

"... ... how much Mike has told you ... ..." Eric trails off, waiting for a response.

I don't give him one.

"About the money?" He's still waiting for a reaction.

"Nothing." At last, my fingers touch a key! I yank it out—but it's our house key. Not the one I'm looking for. "I'm not really interested."

Eric frowns, arms crossed. "Really? You don't ... ... the stealing?"

I knew he was connected to the stealing. I can't ask him. I can't continue the conversation, not if I want him to go away. But man, I wish I could.

He reaches out again, and I leap back. "Don't touch me!" Am I yelling? Maybe someone will hear me. Tears prick the corners of my eyes. Why won't he just go away? "I don't want to have this conversation with you. I don't care about whatever texts you're sending Mike. I want you to leave him alone. And I want you to leave me alone, too." If one more thing goes wrong, I think I'll just scream. Mike. Cam. Eric. The stealing. The library. So many lies.

"Or what?" But he doesn't really say it like a threat, already stepping back, looking down. His hands find his pockets.

"Just go away!" Still no key. I clutch my purse with both hands, ready to fling it at him if he attacks.

"He's a thief," he says, but he's not looking at me anymore.

I don't say anything, just stand very still, like you would if a bear was near you, and hope he goes away.

He mutters something under his breath, scratches the back of his head. And then, without another word, he saunters back toward the curb, opens the door of his truck, and slides in, peeling away so fast his tires spin, the back end of the truck fishtailing before finding purchase.

Thank God.

Ready to give up on finding the key, I push "call" on my phone, hoping the ring will get through to Cam. It doesn't. So, heart still thumping uncomfortably against my tonsils, I admit defeat and upend my purse on the pavement in front of the library. A wad of tissues falls out, along with a handful of ponytail holders, gum wrappers, old keychains without keys attached, my key ring from home, wallet, tic-tacs, and a gift card for Starbucks that I forgot I had. Everything is blurry. I blink back tears. Why did Eric have to show up today? And why are all of my calls going to voicemail? *Pick up, Cam. Please.*

Finally, the library key (on a keychain that Anastasia made using every color of the rainbow and a handful I'm sure she invented herself) topples out. I snatch everything up with two hands, fingers outstretched like claws, dumping it all (even the tissues) back into my purse. I can handle this later. After I find Cam and make sure he's okay. Even Eric is already fading from my mind, unimportant compared to the disappearance of my boyfriend.

The doors stick—of course—so by the time I manage to get them open, wedging my hip in between the two of them so I can shove them apart, I'm sweating. Far in the back of the library, the staff room light is on, but the stacks are dark and quiet as tombs.

"Cam?" I wonder what noises I'm not hearing. If he was calling for help, would my hearing aids pick up the sound of his voice? What if he screamed—telling me to run away?

Every horror movie trailer I've ever seen slings through my imagination at 100kph, and I have to blink assertively to banish them back to my subconscious. This is Golden Sound, not some dark alley in Toronto. But where on earth is Cam?

I call his name again, and this time I'm sure I hear something in return, some faint noise reverberating through the air.

"Where are you?" I reach the staff room and push open the door with my fingertips, expecting to see Cam sprawled across the couch or seated at the table, laptop open in front of him. I don't expect to find him on the floor, bare-chested and breathing hard.

"Are you okay?" I drop to my knees beside him, searching for whatever is hurting him. His skin is slick with sweat, hair plastered to his forehead and the back of his neck, and there are long red welts at his throat, like he clawed his shirt off in a hurry.

Cam coughs, shoulders quivering. He answers me, but between the teeth chattering and the fact that he won't make eye contact, I have no idea what he's saying.

"Cam!" I resist the urge to grab him by the shoulders and shake him until he snaps out of it and instead place both hands on either side of his face, staring straight at him. Is he trembling, or am I? "Cam, what is going on?"

"I'm…okay." He forces the words out, his jaw locked and tense. "Sorry—" He closes his eyes, lips pressed tightly together.

"You don't look okay." I'm just stating a fact, but after the words leave my mouth, I realize they're definitely not the most helpful thing I could have said right now. I release Cam's face and reach for his hands instead, but he pulls away from me.

"I just need some space," he says, throat constricting like it's hard to speak or breathe, like there isn't enough air in the room. "I just need, like—can you step back? A little?" He's practically panting, one hand twitching toward his throat again, the other pressed against his chest.

"Where does it hurt?"

He coughs again. "Heart. My heart."

With the hand not fisted into his own chest, he reaches for his wrist—which is lacking a watch, I see now, the fingertips of his free hand cracked and bleeding.

He's way too young to be having a heart attack. But the pain on his face is real. When Mom was a teenager, she said she had panic attacks from the stress at school. She swore it felt like she was having a stroke, or an asthma attack, or losing her mind.

I never got it. How could your body lie to you that much? Either your heart's working or it's not. Either you can breathe, or you can't. But now, looking at Cam, it all makes perfect sense to me. "You're okay," I say, slowly, sitting down with my back against the wall a few feet away.

Cam's chest heaves. "I know." But he doesn't look convinced, the pain evident in the tiny wrinkles at the corner of each eye. He winces every few seconds, fist pressing more firmly against his breastbone like he can punch his own heart into submission.

"Where's your watch?" I try to keep my voice low and smooth, imagining myself spooning words out like molasses, slow and serene.

He winces again, forcing the words out past lips so stiff they look like they're made of concrete. "Broken." He points in the general direction of the table, and when I lean over, I see his discarded watch, the band snapped completely in half.

"What happened?"

Cam's breathing is coming easier now, the heaving of his chest calmed down to short inhalations and exhalations, rather than the explosive heaving he was doing when I walked in. He wipes his forehead with the back of his hand, sighs, and then shivers. "Where's my shirt?" I reach for it on the couch and toss it to him. He towels off with it briskly and then yanks it over his head before climbing to his feet and collapsing on the couch, head resting in his hands.

I get up off the floor and sit beside him, resting my head on his shoulder. I wait, hoping he'll tell me what's going on without prompting.

"My watch," he says after a minute, staring down at the broken band in my hands. "I didn't notice when it snapped. I just heard it hit the floor."

I turn it over in my hands, but the face isn't shattered. Just the band, snapped raggedly in two. When he doesn't say anything else for a minute or two, I sit back where I can see him better, keeping one hand on his back.

As if in answer to a question, he nods. "I got here a few hours ago."

I wait.

"I had a nightmare," he says, "that the library got shut down and Ana came back to visit and sobbed in my arms. And then I woke up and I had to…I don't know. Do something."

"What *did* you do?" I survey the staff room. It looks the same.

"Research," he says, rubbing his forehead. "Tried starting up an Instagram page and an online petition. Stuff like that."

"And the panic attack?" I am not about to pretend that didn't happen. "When did that start?"

He looks like he's going to deny it, eyebrows coming firm and low on his forehead, but the sight of the watch stops him. "When you texted."

My heart stutters like I've been punched in the chest. "Me?"

He's not looking at me, staring at his hands as he nods. "Not you, you know? Just the realization that I didn't have anything to show you. I didn't accomplish anything. We're still stuck in a los-ing battle. I wanted to fix it for you. With everything that's gone wrong—Mike—I wanted to do something right."

I try to focus on the *Not you, you know?* so I can stop hearing him say *when you texted*, but the association burns me. "I don't need you to fix it for me." I lean into him, hoping he'll make eye contact with me.

He turns his face toward me so I can read his lips, but he's looking over my shoulder, his gaze far away. "It doesn't matter," he says, the word shapes soft on his lips, like he's whispering. "I wanted to."

"You shouldn't feel so responsible for this." I squeeze his arm. "Cam. I'm serious. The library is just a library. Ana is off living her own life with her sister and her kid. I'm only here because I care about *you*."

"I'm tired of the big guy always winning." He sighs. "I don't ... ... let her down. Or you." He's staring at his hands.

"It's not important." I would raze this whole building to the ground to save Cam. "Not as important as you."

He wipes his face with the neck of his shirt, shakes his head. Heaves out a sigh. "I really thought we could do it. I thought we could convince them."

"We're done." I touch his neck with my fingertips. "Cam?"

He glances over at me.

"We're done trying to save the library." I nod as I say it, like my own affirmation will convince him.

"Skylar." Cam shakes his head, and I see him trying to pull it together, trying to straighten his shoulders and get it all under control, say something calming, look at me with those gentle eyes. "We can't. There's too much at stake. Too many people invested to give it up now."

"Cam." I feel my voice crack before I realize I have tears in my eyes. "We are not fighting to the death over this if the only one dying is you."

"The town loves this library," he says, crossing his wrists over his chest in the sign for LOVE. "I love this library."

"But I love you." I say the words without planning to, but when I feel them on my lips, I release them without hesitation. "And I would do anything to keep you safe."

Cam softens, his face crumpling at the edges the way paper falls in on itself as it's burning, eyes squeezed shut, one hand half over his face. And even though I have no idea if you're supposed to hug someone recovering from a panic attack, I reach for him and he falls into me, forehead pressed into my shoulder.

He mumbles something, mouth pressed against my shirt, and I rub my hand down his back, damp with sweat. Did I just miss my first *I love you, too*?

When he pulls back, swiping roughly at his eyes with the back of his hand, I pass him the tissues. He blows his nose violently and tosses the box onto the couch between us.

"Skylar."

"Hm?"

He looks me full in the face for the first time since I showed up. His eyes are bloodshot and the skin around them is baggy. His cheeks are flushed, damp hair plastered to the sides of his face. But the way he looks at me reminds me of Aiden, and I think I must know what he looked like as a child. There's something of a little boy about him again.

"I don't know what I would do without you." Cam clears his throat, like there are more tears still trapped back there somewhere. He reaches for my hand, twining our fingers together. "You know I love you, right?"

I go warm all over, like I've stepped into a hot tub and sunk down all the way to my neck.

"I so love you," he says, and then pulls me in for a kiss, soft lips pressed to mine like he's okay and we have all the time in the world and who cares about the library, anyway, at this point?

"I know," I whisper back when we pull free of each other. And I did know—but I'm so glad I heard him say it out loud.

"We can do this." He says it like a question.

"Should we?"

We stare at each other across the couch.

"If it's going to…" I want to say *affect you like this*, but that sounds like I'm scolding. "…stress you out?"

Cam shakes his head. "I have to do this."

"But why?" I plant my hands on his knees, studying him like I'll find the answers in the tilt of his eyebrows or the freckles on his cheeks. "Why, Cam? It's just a library. Let someone else champion it for a little while."

He's still shaking his head. "It's not that. I just picture Ana's face on the phone. Or the knitting club when I tell them they can't meet. Or the kids' story time play group. And then all I can think about is the board members thinking they're doing us all a favour by shutting it down. Thinking we're too hick to know better."

I feather my words out like a breath of wind. "But is it worth it?" I clench my fingers around his watch, the tiny dial on the side pressing uncomfortably into my skin.

"I have to do this." He's reaching for the computer even as he says it. His hands are shaking.

I snatch it and cradle it on my lap, out of his reach. At least for now. "Okay."

He raises an eyebrow like he's teasing, but the tension in his jaw says maybe his teeth are chattering and he doesn't want me to know. "Okay?"

"I'll help you get the library back." But even though he stretches his hand out for the laptop, I don't give it back. "On one condition."

He waits. "And that condition is…"

"I need you to tell me, truthfully, that if this doesn't work, you'll be okay."

He winces.

"Tell me you believe you're worth more than your success or failure, and I'm in. I'm in all the way."

Cam stares at his hands, thinking.

The laptop is warm on my lap.

"What if I said I'm not there yet?" He shoots a sideways glance at me. "But I'll work on it? For real, this time."

"Cam." I grab his hand. "What if we fail?"

At least this time, he doesn't flinch.

"Look me in the eyes and say we'd be okay." Please.

He makes firm eye contact with me and squeezes my hand. "If we fail..." His throat hitches. "...we'll be okay." He must see the concern still on my face, because he adds, "Skylar, I promise."

Chapter
EIGHTEEN
Mike

AFTER DROPPING SKYLAR OFF AT THE LIBRARY, IT TAKES GETTING STUCK AT the red light at the end of the street for me to realize that it's almost an hour before I'm supposed to be at camp. With the flashing hand counting down from thirty (just my luck) I pull out my phone and text my sister. *Hope everything's ok. Sorry again about the social media pages.*

I expect her to text back right away, but when the light turns green again without a text back, I toss my phone into the passenger seat and make a left turn towards Aunt Kay's house. I need some time to think. I drive the few minutes to my aunt's, planning to just sit in the driveway until I'm within at least a half hour of the start of my shift. When I pull in, though, my aunt is sitting on the porch wearing sweatpants and a tank top, her hair piled in a stack on top of her head. She waves enthusiastically when she sees the car, so I turn it off and get out, waving back.

"What a nice surprise!" Aunt Kay walks across the porch toward me. "After last night, I wasn't sure you'd come back!"

"Well." I meet her at the steps and shrug. "Here I am." The words feel harsh leaving my mouth, so I pull my lips back into a smile.

"I'm sorry, Micah. I know I don't have the lightest touch in the world." She shakes her head, making her hair quiver. "You must be on your way to work. It's awfully early."

"I dropped Skylar off at the library to work on something with Cam."

"Can you stay for a little while?" She beckons me toward the porch chairs. "Come and tell me what's on your mind after last night."

"I'm okay."

She throws a look over her shoulder as she climbs the steps. "You have your dad's face, remember?"

Right. Thanks, Dad. "No, it's nothing, really." I sit down across from her and let her pour me a cup of iced tea. Was she just sitting out here with two glasses?

Aunt Kay looks up and catches me looking. "Oh, this?" She hands me a glass. "I like to be prepared in case one of the neighbors pops by."

"Do they do that often?" I take a sip. It's already hot out here.

"Sometimes." Aunt Kay sits back in her chair.

I can just *tell* she wants to ask if I've called my parents. But, to her credit, she doesn't say anything.

"Skylar and I are going to talk later." About school, for sure. And, if I'm brave enough, Eric, too.

"That's good." Aunt Kay nods encouragingly. But even she doesn't know about Eric.

"Sometimes I feel like I'm playing whack-a-mole with my life." I choke out a laugh that hurts my throat. "Every time I solve one problem, another one pops up. It's like, I know I should do better, but I just can't get there."

Aunt Kay listens, hands wrapped around her glass of iced tea. She nods slowly, but she doesn't say anything.

"Will I ever feel like I've done enough? Do you think, after I've figured this all out, I'll go back to feeling..." I shake my head, searching for the word. "Normal?"

Aunt Kay sighs, tracing the condensation droplets with her fingertips. "One of my favorite books is about a boy who turns into a dragon."

"What?" I take a drink of my own iced tea to mask my frustration. I'm talking about real life. Why is she bringing kids' stories into it?

"He wants to be human again, like his friends," she continues, ignoring my question. "So he does everything he can think of to be 'good.' He helps other people. He apologizes for his mistakes. But it doesn't make him human."

This sounds vaguely familiar. "What does?"

"All of his hard work can't change his heart," my aunt says, sitting back. "Instead, a lion comes—"

Now I know why I recognize this story. "Is this from that movie? The Chronicles of Narnia?"

"It was a book first," she says, raising her pointer finger. "But yes, you're right. The lion is the only one who can turn him back into a boy again. He acted good, but he couldn't change on his own. He needed a little help."

"You sound like Skylar."

Aunt Kay shrugs. "I'm not trying to tell you what to believe, Micah. I'm just saying, if you want something you can't achieve on your own, maybe it's time to explore other options."

This is the second time she's brought this up. What does it mean? I finish my tea and spin the glass in my hands, suddenly tired. Whack-a-mole, man. Everything has a second step to it. I just want answers.

"What time are you supposed to be at work?" Aunt Kay checks her watch. "Nine o'clock?"

"Ahh, shoot!" I leap to my feet. "Sorry, Aunt Kay. I'll see you later."

"Good luck!" She shoos me off the porch with both hands.

I leap into the car and throw it into gear, reversing as quickly as I safely can down the driveway. Once I turn onto the country roads, I realize it's not so bad. I won't be early, but I'm probably not going to be late. In fact, I pull into the parking lot with two minutes to spare. I grab my phone, lock the car from the fob, and jog all the way into the building, past Lily's spot at the front desk and into my classroom.

The kids are all milling around, some still filing in, but Emily is already seated and playing her ukulele. Her tiny fingers stretch to the max just to cover all the chords. She's caught her tongue between her teeth, concentrating hard, and even though the other kids are squirming in their seats, eager to get started with the day, I don't address them. Not until she's done.

Something about her face reminds me of Skylar when we were kids, always desperate to one-up me, tag along on my adventures, do everything I could do, and do it better. We're only a year apart, but sometimes I felt like I was a lot older. By the time we were ten, I knew she was looking to me for approval. I don't know how much she looks up to me anymore.

"Well?" She finishes with a flourish, pick clenched in her fist as she holds one hand high in triumph.

"That was really good." I have to shake myself back to the present.

She waits.

I clear my throat. "Excellent handshape, nice and relaxed all the way to the end." I try to remember the last few bars. Dang. I got distracted. "Can anyone tell me something that Emily did well?"

Hands fly into the air, the class eager to please and tired of sitting still. I call on them at random, nodding along as they share, some of their stories veering away from the guitar and into their daily lives or what happened during the afternoon session yesterday. I can't focus. Maybe Aunt Kay is right. Maybe I need a little bit of help. And maybe Skylar can help me figure out where to find it.

At last, the clock turns twelve thirty. And, at the same instant, my phone lights up with a text.

"Okay, class." It feels like I'm speaking through a cotton ball. "Time for lunch. Grab your backpacks and head to the gym."

They disappear almost instantly. My phone feels hot in my hand as the door slams shut behind Emily, who always takes extra care putting her uke in its case.

It's my sister, responding to my text from this morning.

Cam's ok. Sort of. We're figuring it out. can we talk soon?

I fumble my way through the rest of the afternoon session, giving the students such long practice sessions that I see them slouch in their seats. But the conversation we're about to have is at the forefront of my mind. I just want to get started.

I drive home with my mind whirling with everything Aunt Kay has said and all my own plans for honesty. Where to start? What to say first? Will this conversation fix everything? Or is there something else I'm missing?

I'm hoping to catch my sister back at the house, but Cam and Skylar are together all evening, and Skylar makes no move to leave him.

• • •

I wait in the kitchen for Skylar to come down the next morning, hoping she'll want to go for a run. I eat my banana as slowly as I can, stretching out my calves, but she doesn't show up. Cam's parents wander through the kitchen, brew coffee, and wander out, whispering *hello* and *good morning* like without caffeine, they're only operating at 50% power. Even Cam comes down in his pajamas, purple circles under his eyes.

He glances around the kitchen. "Skylar?"

I shake my head.

She finally drags herself downstairs almost an hour later than normal, kisses Cam on the cheek, and flops into the seat next to him at the kitchen table. She looks exhausted, like someone's wrung her out overnight and hung her out to dry.

"Did you not sleep well?" I drop a Pop-Tart in front of her, but she's not looking at me and jumps when it hits the table.

"Geez, Mike," she mumbles, her words thicker than normal, and quiet. She doesn't have her hearing aids in.

Frustration rises in me—today, when I need to talk to her, why is she in such a weird mood?—but I know I'm not being fair. I haven't wanted to talk to her in ages. She can return the favor if she wants to. I tap my fingers on the table in front of her and wait until she squints up at me.

"Want to go for a run?" I say it slow, making sure to enunciate.

She sits up a little straighter, rubbing her forehead like she's got a headache. "Now?" Her free hand twitches toward the table, thumb and pinky outstretched, palm turned to the sky.

"Sure." I shrug like I haven't been pacing the kitchen for the past two hours. Waiting for her.

Cam finishes his bowl of cereal, holding his spoon between fingers covered in Band-Aids. Skylar shoots a sideways glance at him. He doesn't notice, rising to set his bowl in the sink, but I watch her watch him as he stretches by the counter. She looks away before he can turn back around.

"Okay." She rises, too, apparently satisfied by whatever she's seen—or maybe what she hasn't—in Cam. "Let me get my shoes."

• ● •

When we finally make it outside, jogging lightly down the driveway to the road, she doesn't say much.

"How are things going with Cam?" I should just say it and get it over with, but the truth about last summer, school, the internship, all of it—when did it get to be so much?—feels stuck in the back of my throat.

Skylar wooshes out a sigh. I feel her exhale against the side of my face, and I have to hold back a flinch that would send me into the middle of the road.

"He's…" She searches for the words. "I don't know, Mike. The social media thing really caught us both off-guard. We were kind of counting on having, like, a million people online backing us up."

Is this my chance? Should I say something now?

Skylar keeps talking before I can interject. "And then to find out that we don't, after all—and we've been promising everyone that we had it covered—and this stupid board and their stupid plans for this town that half of them don't even live in!"

I touch her arm, trying to get her to slow down without scaring her. She's sending words off into the wind like they've been stacking up inside her for ages.

For a few minutes, we run in silence. Skylar is almost panting, her shoulders heaving. I know what it feels like to have those days—like you're running through peanut butter instead of air. I hate running on days like that. Usually, I stop after a few blocks and jog home. But Skylar seems determined to run herself back into a good place. Or into the ground. It's difficult to tell what she's aiming for.

"I don't know, Mike."

Right when I think she's going to slow to a walk, she leaps into a sprint. She must really be having a bad day, because I catch her in just a few strides, swinging my arms to keep pace with her when normally, she can leave me in the dust.

"I'll tell you anything you need to know." I pass her so she can see me, and then drop to a walk. "What do you need?"

Skylar stops walking, puts her hands on her knees, and ducks her head, shoulders heaving. "I want answers," she says, her voice shaky. "How come no one can ever just give me answers?"

I know what it feels like to ask that question. And I have a funny feeling she's not just talking about the library anymore. "I don't know." I wrap an arm around her shoulders. "And I'm sorry. For my part in this. In fact—"

"I feel like we've tried everything." She must not have heard me. "And it's not enough. And then there's you, and Eric, and whatever happened last summer."

Here it is. I open my mouth to tell her, but she's still talking.

"He said something about you…but then I went into the library and found Cam, and I don't know, Mike. I don't think it's going to work. I think we're going to lose it."

And the moment for telling my own story has passed again.

"I need a new idea." She turns to look at me. "I know you're switching programs, but did you learn anything at all in any of your classes that might help? Anything?"

"People need to feel that they have buy-in," I say slowly, turning ideas over in my brain, trying to think of something that will help. "They need to be convinced that keeping the library will benefit them in some way. They need to have a stake in the game somehow. And you can have the bonus of using their buy-in to convince whoever you need to convince that the town cares enough to make this worthwhile."

"We could make signs!" She tugs the end of her braid over her shoulder and pulls the hair apart, thinking.

"I don't think that will be enough on its own." I did, at least, learn that much.

"Why is nothing ever enough?" Skylar grips the hair at the sides of her head in an exaggerated grimace. At least I think it's an exaggeration. "Mike, I don't know what else to do."

"You need awareness." Before she can open her eyes to glare at me, I hurry on. "Social media flopped. But old-fashioned news still carries a lot of weight. See if you can get any big-city newspapers interested in the cause. Get some university campus activists on your side. Create a public outcry bigger than the people of Golden Sound."

Skylar nods along, thinking. "We could sell them signs, too. All proceeds go towards whatever it would cost to change their plans and build their big fancy YMCA at the other location."

I hope this works. "You could try."

"I have to tell Cam!" Skylar spins mid-stride, jogging back toward the house without waiting to see if I'm keeping up.

"Come on." I have to pull slightly ahead of her to make sure she can read my lips. "Let's finish the run first." If I can figure out a way to change the subject, I can still tell her about Eric.

"I'm done." She shakes me off without a second glance. "Come on, Mike! Cam's been looking for a breakthrough for so long. This will…" she flounders, looking for the right word, "…absolutely *thrill* him! I can't wait to see the look on his face!" And she puts on another burst of speed, her run no longer sagging and tired. Instead, she looks like she's hit her second wind.

No matter how much I try, I can't pump my arms hard enough to pull ahead of her again, and every attempt to call her name is lost in the wind. Skylar keeps her eyes forward, like she's running back to Cam instead of just finishing off our morning jog. She doesn't even slow to a walk at the opening of the driveway where we normally start our cool-down, so I stop without her and watch her sprint toward the house, leaping up the steps and flinging open the front door. She's hollering for Cam, her voice drifting back to me on the wind.

And she still doesn't know the truth. I try to fit sentences together in my head—I'll ask to talk to her privately, take her out on the porch, and tell her there—but when I walk through the front door, she and Cam are sitting side-by-side on the couch, their heads bent over his laptop. They're talking too fast to follow, both of their hands throwing in an occasional sign, pointing at the computer screen. Neither one of them notices me head up the stairs.

I figure I'll shower and try to talk to her again, but when I come downstairs, they've moved to the table. Skylar's hair is swept up on top of her head, the back of her tank top still soaked with sweat.

"Hey." I nudge the back of her head with the tips of my fingers, and she glances up.

"Mike!" She half-stands, looks like she wants to say something, and then stops, chewing her lip. "Can we talk?"

I nod. "I'm free now—"

"Sometime soon? In a few hours, maybe?" She glances back down at the table. "Cam, what if we had people stake the signs in their front lawns? Like they do when there's an election?"

He nods, reaching for a paper and pen. "Like this, right?" He sketches something out loosely in front of them, and Skylar snatches it up and scrutinizes it, our conversation already forgotten.

I leave the kitchen before things get any weirder, letting myself out the front door and breathing in the quiet air of the front porch. Maybe Skylar isn't the person I need to be talking to. Maybe if I want to clear the air, the person I really need to confess to is Alex.

I turn around and go back inside before I can change my mind. Skylar and Cam don't even look up, heads still bowed over their work. I pad quietly up the stairs, pull my keys out of the pocket of yesterday's shorts, and pause in the doorway, bracing my hands against the doorframe. *Do I really want to do this?*

I can't change my mind. I don't want to chicken out again. So I stop thinking, force myself through the doorway, and jog down the stairs. I hit the kitchen at a jog, not even glancing at Skylar and Cam, and fling open the front door. I need to get to the car before my sense of self-preservation returns. And then I just have to keep my foot glued to the accelerator all the way into town.

Aunt Kay's dragon story pops into my head again. Will telling Alex change anything for me? Or do I have to find a lion of my own to finally feel free again?

I turn the radio on as loud as I can, once I'm safely on the country roads and away from distractions, too far away to be called back by a curious wave from the porch. The sound feels heavy against my eardrums, vibrating through the floor of the car and causing the wing mirrors to tremble. The bass thumps in my chest, next to my heartbeat, and because half of my attention is going to breathing (the other half is focused on the road), I don't have any room left to hear myself think for a change.

• ● •

The Golden Sound town sign appears far too quickly on the horizon, and although I have to reluctantly lower the volume of the radio, I don't slow my speed. When I hit the 50kph warning sign, I slam on the brakes, feeling the seat belt tighten across my chest. Anything to distract me. Anything to keep myself going, as fast as I can, to the coffee shop. To Alex.

The streets are open and empty, and I have no trouble pulling into a spot on the street in front of the tattoo parlor. I don't bother paying for a ticket. I'll take the fine. I just have to get in there.

I forget to check both ways before crossing the street, but the only car on the road simply slows, the driver waving as he passes. Like I was stopping to say hello. And then the tattoo parlor door is in front of me, the cool metal handle thick and heavy in my palm.

I yank it open too hard and the bell shrills over my head, the glass door slamming into the wall, despite my efforts to catch it and pull it back. Alex's head pops over the counter, eyes wide.

"Sorry." An apt way to begin this conversation. I close the door softly behind me, stepping up to the counter.

"Hi, Mike." She looks less tired today, the wrinkles around her eyes looking more like smile memories than anything else. "What can I get you?"

I clear my throat to force back the coffee order that jumps to mind. My last chance to escape the truth. "Actually, I wanted to talk to you for a minute. If that's okay."

She leans her elbows on the counter. "Sure, that's no problem. It's always slow right after we open. The lunch-break crowd won't be here for another hour."

A tattoo pen buzzes in the back room, the low chatter of the artist and client silhouetted against the jazz music coming from Alex's Bluetooth speaker.

I clear my throat again. "About the job last summer."

Alex frowns.

"This won't take long," I assure her. "And it's not about you."

"Okay." She steps back, wipes her hands on her apron, like she needs a few extra inches between us before she can listen to me speak.

"Please." I cross my arms over my chest, but when she takes another half-step back, I let them hang loosely by my sides instead. "I just wanted to apologize."

"What for?"

Deep breath. "I know you didn't take the money last summer."

She waits, wiping her already-clean hands down her apron over and over again.

"Because I did."

Her mouth falls open.

"It was stupid." And so is this. Why did I think coming here would make anything better? I don't have the money to give back. I don't have anything to offer. What good is an apology going to do after the damage I've done? "One of the stupidest things I've ever done. I quit after you got fired. And I'm sorry."

"But if you knew..." Alex's hands bury deep in her apron pockets. "If you knew, why didn't you say anything? You were there when I got fired. I remember seeing you by the register. Why didn't you tell him it wasn't me?"

We stare at each other across the counter. I have no answer.

She sighs, long and heavy. "Okay. Is that all?"

She wants me to leave. "I was a coward." I drop the word like a brick between us. "And now I'm trying to make it right."

Alex covers her eyes with her hand like she needs a break, a moment of privacy. From behind her hand, she asks, "What did you do with the money?"

I wince, even though she can't see me. "Spent it. On alcohol. And weed."

She huffs out a tiny laugh. "Oh my gosh."

"I'm sorry." I feel worse. I thought this might help, might make me feel better, but it just feels like I've tangled an already knotted string, stirred a boiled-over pot. This isn't helping anyone. "Is there anything I can do?"

"Oh my gosh," she says again. When she takes her hand away from her face, her eyes are wet.

I made her cry. I jam my hands in my pockets, searching for tissues. I have none. I don't know where to look. I don't know what to say. I end up just staring at the floor, hoping she'll sniff it back instead of progressing into full-on sobs.

"I really needed that job," she whispers, using the edge of her sleeve to dab the corners of her eyes. "And it was so embarrass-ing—"

I can only nod.

"—and I had to go home and explain to my daughter." She shakes her head. "They've still got me on probation here. Curse of a small town is something like this hangs over you forever. Every-one knows. No one will ever forget." She heaves out a sigh.

"I'll tell McDonald's the truth." The words escape me before I realize I'm going to say them. Can I follow through with this? "Or your boss here. Whatever you want."

Alex pulls down a paper cup and rolls it between the palms of her hands. "Okay. Yeah, that would help."

"Do you need anything else?" I wish I could give her some-thing. Some token or tangible proof that would erase the pain of last summer. You'd think by now I would have learned that pain can't be erased. Just survived.

She shakes her head. "Just this job. And maybe a raise." It sounds like a joke, but clearly isn't.

"I'll call McDonald's tonight." I wonder if it's too soon to start edging toward the door.

Alex folds her arms. "Was it just you? Or was it that other guy, too? Eric?"

I shrug. Until yesterday, I'd have thrown him under the bus in a heartbeat. But I can't stop thinking about him slamming his fist into the concrete. Not even feeling the pain. And I think, what good would it do now?

"Right," she says. "I never liked him, you know."

I did. Back when I thought his method worked. But I think telling her that would only make things worse.

As the silence stretches uncomfortably long, Alex clears her throat. "Can I get you anything? Or did you just come for the apologies?" She can't quite make eye contact with me, her gaze focused just over my shoulder.

I don't blame her. "I'm sorry."

She nods, tight-lipped and trembling. An older couple opens the door, bell tinkling overhead, and she clears her throat and turns to greet them. "Thanks for coming in."

I duck out past the couple, rolling my neck when I hit the sidewalk. I thought I'd feel lighter, but it feels exactly like it did just a few minutes ago. Messy. Unresolved.

I still really need to talk to Skylar. I wish she could talk on the phone. I make it back to the car and roll the windows down, turning the car off but leaving the key in the ignition. And then I call Cam.

"Hello?" His voice sounds muffled, like he's got the phone pinned between his shoulder and his ear. "Is everything okay?"

I clear my throat. "Yeah, I'm good. I just wanted to pass on a message for Skylar."

"He wants to talk to you," Cam says. "Okay." This is to me again. "What's up?"

"Can you ask her if she's free when I get home?"

Cam repeats this message. Skylar says, "What? Why? Where is he now?"

"I heard her."

Cam waits for me to answer.

"I'll tell her everything when I get back."

"Okay," says Cam. "Sounds good. See you soon?"

"Yeah. Thanks."

"No problem."

Skylar's saying something in the background when I disconnect the call, wrapping both hands around the steering wheel. Talking to Alex was one thing, but the conversation that scares me the most is the one I'm about to have with my little sister.

Chapter
NINETEEN
Skylar

"DO YOU REALLY THINK PEOPLE WILL BUY THESE?" I FLOP DOWN NEXT TO Cam and his drawing of the signs we want to sell to people to put up in their yards.

SAVE OUR LIBRARY, reads one side, and EMAIL THE BOARD TODAY is printed on the other.

"Only if they know about them," he says. "Did you email the newspaper?"

"Your local and my local." I tick them off my fingers. "And I texted Ana and asked her to reach out to her local paper, too."

"I think it's missing something," says Cam, scrutinizing it with his head tilted to one side. "Like, a drawing of some kind. What do you think?"

I crane my neck to look out the window, even though Mike hung up the phone approximately thirty seconds ago and I know there's no way he's home already. "Yes. Definitely."

"Skylar." Cam leaves his seat at the table, puts an arm around my waist, and tugs me gently back toward my chair. "You didn't even look at it."

"Did he say what he wanted to talk about?" I blink at the sketch on the table. It looks fine to me. But I'm terrible at anything artsy, so that's not saying much.

"I already told you he just said he wanted to talk to you." Cam points toward the sign again. "Pretend you're one of Beth's knitting club ladies. What would you want the sign to say?"

The look on his face is everything I've ever wanted. Excited, not anxious. Hopeful, not defeated. And I swallow back everything I was about to say.

My brother is important. But he's not the *only* important person in my life. And right now, Cam doesn't seem to notice he's not wearing a watch, his fingers looked less swollen when he changed the Band-Aids this morning, and I caught him scrolling through his personal Instagram over breakfast instead of drafting emails to the mayor.

So I close my eyes and force Mike out of my head so I can think like a knitting lady. And after only a few minutes, my frantic sense of Mike-induced panic has eased. Like by forcing myself to adopt a new perspective, I believe in it. Just a little bit.

"Well?" Cam doodles in pencil on top of one of the drawings.

The new mindset has done absolutely nothing for my creativity. "All I can think of is knitting needles."

He rolls his eyes. "We can't put knitting needles on library signs. We need something universal."

"Books?"

Cam groans, sinking his head into his hands. "We're doomed."

"What?" I actually thought the books were kind of a good idea, but maybe that's just too obvious? "I wish we could just let everyone design their own. That way we wouldn't miss anyone, and the library would be super well-represented."

"Hey." He lifts his head, a thoughtful look on his face. "That's not such a bad idea."

"A design-your-own library sign campaign?" I don't see how this is different than us selling the blank signs we ourselves would be ordering online.

"Not exactly." Cam leans over the paper, sketching it all out. He's mumbling away, but when he looks up and catches my pleading glance, he repeats himself for me, "What about a fill-in-the-blank. 'I love my library because _____'"

"That could work!" I picture a sea of signs set up on lawns, a million reasons to keep the library open. To keep Cam happy. To make Ana proud.

Cam's examining the online order form when the front door opens and Mike, who I forgot to worry about these past twenty minutes, walks in. He looks like he sucked up everything that's been bothering Cam these past few weeks: his eyes are heavy and lined and his shoulders stoop, like his backpack has more than just his wallet inside.

"Can we … … somewhere quiet … … talk?" He doesn't even say hi, just jerks his chin toward the living room.

Cam is too engrossed in the sign order to look up and catch my confused expression. No moral support from that corner, I guess. It's not like I should need it, anyway. It's just Mike. But the last time we had a serious living room talk, I found out a whole lot about him—and the accident—that I didn't know before. And this feels like exactly the same type of conversation.

"What's up?" I blurt it out even before we're seated on the couch, each at one end. I lean back on the armrest, feet curled up underneath me. Mike leans forward so he can rest his elbows on his knees. "Is this about school? And the social media platforms?"

He hesitates. "Not exactly. I mean, we can talk about that if you want to. I'm sorry I didn't tell you sooner. I should have. And I don't expect you to forgive me—"

"I'm mad at you." I point a finger at him. "Really. I still don't know why you didn't just talk to me. But I do forgive you. I want you to know that." After all, he's still my brother. I want him to be okay. I want him to be happy. I so badly want him to find the forgiveness I've experienced. The love that chased me down last summer and keeps reaching me in new ways a year later.

Mike's eyebrows shoot up. "I don't deserve it."

"You've got that right."

He winces.

"No, that's not what I meant." How has this conversation gotten out of hand already? "I mean, yeah, you screwed up. But I love you. There's not much you could do that would change that."

Mike clears his throat. "Well, maybe you'll change your mind after you hear the rest of it."

The rest of what?

"I've got some stuff to tell you, and I need you to listen all the way through without interrupting."

"Is it Eric again?" I was hoping maybe he dropped off the face of the earth. Or died. Is it bad that the idea of that brings me a serious amount of relief?

Mike hesitates. My stomach plummets into my feet.

"Not like that," he says, hastily. "He is involved. But this is about last summer."

I listen without saying anything as he tells me about McDonald's. The barista named Alex who used to work there. The stolen money. Eric. The comments about Mike being a thief make sense now. Why can't my brother make a good decision for once in his life?

"So I went to see Alex this morning," he says, and I can tell by the exhaustion in his eyes that he's coming to the end of his story. "And I thought talking to her would make me feel better, but it didn't. And I wondered why until I realized I don't really care what she thinks of me. We live in totally different towns. We lead different lives. What does it matter if she knows I was an idiot the summer after high school?"

"Okay—"

He shakes his head, holding up a hand to stop me. "Let me finish, okay?"

I zip my lips shut.

"This whole thing." He shakes his head again. "The only reason

Eric had anything to hold over me in the first place is because of how much I didn't want to tell you the truth." He stares down at his hands, fingers spread. "It was hanging over my head like some kind of threat. After last summer, I didn't want to be that guy anymore. And I didn't want you to see me like that, either. But I keep making mistakes. I keep being that person, and I just could never work up the courage to tell you the truth. Things kept getting worse. I'm sorry I'm not the person I used to be for everyone, but I'm just not. I can't keep living under everyone's worry and disappointment, and I just don't know what to do about it." He sighs. "So that's it. That's all of it."

I hold my breath for a minute, thinking. It's like a wave has crashed over me, and I don't know which way is up.

"You don't have to say anything right away." Mike looks down at his hands. "It's a lot. I know."

I nod. Alex—Eric—school—what?

"I'm so sorry," he whispers.

"Mike." I rest a hand on his knee. "Look at me."

He drags his chin up, eyes barely meeting my face.

"I don't see you like that." I wish there was a way to promise so he'd believe me. "Mike. Really."

"I feel like I've been this guy for such a long time, Skylar." Mike buries his face in his hands, but lifts it before continuing so I can read his lips. "Not just this year. Not even since the accident. I had questions before, too. And I'm afraid, no matter what I do, I'll never be able to find what I'm missing. Figure out how to be a good person again."

I shift on the couch, replaying his words in my mind to make sure I've heard him right. "Wait, what are you missing?"

He shakes his head. "Something Aunt Kay said made me think. And there's this kids' song from camp I just can't get out of my head."

I hold my breath, waiting for an explanation.

Mike closes his eyes. "Look, Skylar." He cracks them open

again, flushing. "I'm not converting, okay? And I definitely don't want to come to church with you or anything. But I have some questions. If you don't mind trying to answer them sometime."

I suck in a breath and almost choke. "Are you serious?"

"Don't make a big deal out of it." He runs a hand over the back of his head, ducking so I can't quite see his face.

God, thank you! I imagine that prayer going heavenward with about a million exclamation marks after it. "Do you want to start now? Do you have any questions you want me to answer?"

"Not today." Mike stands up. "I've still got a few more things to do to make this right."

The look on his face makes me think I'm hearing Mike for the very first time. Even my hearing aids can't mask the honesty seeping through every tiny flicker in his expression.

"That's it. That's all I wanted to say." He stands up. "Thanks for listening." He doesn't ask me not to tell our parents. I wonder if he wants me to. I wonder if he will.

"What...happens now?" I was going to say *what are you going to do now*, but that feels too much like an accusation.

"I'm going to McDonald's." He swings his car keys around his finger. "Alex doesn't want the job back, but they should know the truth. Stop the rumours about her."

"You're doing the right thing." I look him in the eyes, and when he meets my gaze he looks, for the first time in forever, like he's listening to something other than whatever lies play inside his head. All those months I spent trying to get through to him, and all he had to do was choose to do the right thing. It was that simple.

Or maybe it was that difficult.

"Thanks, Skylar." He stretches out a long arm and pulls me into a side hug, resting his cheek on the top of my head.

I wrap both arms around him and squeeze, trying to give him strength and tell him I love him and I'm so, so proud—without using words.

He croaks something out after a few seconds—I can feel his

ribcage contract when he protests—and I release him, stepping back. "Okay. Go. You can do this."

"I'll be back later," he says, and ducks into the entryway.

I trail after him, looking for Cam in the kitchen, but a flurry of movement by the front door catches my eye. Someone's arm waving, maybe? Light filtering through the trees? Whatever it was, I'm distracted from the kitchen (which is empty, anyway) and follow Mike to the door. Cam's standing there, too, and with him is a short, blonde lady, her curls piled high on the very top of her head—

"Ana?" Her name barely escapes my lips before she's flying at me like an arrow destined for the bullseye, wrapping her arms around my waist, her face buried in my shoulder. She chatters away into thin air, and when I find Cam, grinning broadly as he looks at us, he shakes his head.

HAPPY, he signs, open palms circling over his torso, and I know I'm not missing anything.

"I missed you," I choke out when she releases me. "Ana, what are you doing here?"

Anastasia cups my face in her hands, beaming. "I came to visit! I couldn't … … back to Golden Sound … … not come say hello!"

Before I can get a word in edgewise, she continues, refusing to stand still long enough for me to lipread a complete sentence.

"I told Sophia that after … … stress of moving … … finding a house and having to stay … … basement … … weeks—which I really don't recommend, for … … of reasons—all I really wanted … … was come and … … things were going here."

Ana continues talking, but over her shoulder, I see Cam's face. Can we tell her our plan? Will it really be enough?

When I tune in again to Ana, I have no idea what she's talking about anymore. She mentions something about Nutella (I think?) and then launches into some sort of list, ticking items off on her fingers.

Cam steps forward—saved by the boyfriend!—a worried pucker between his eyebrows. "Ana, about the library—"

She shakes out her curls and then piles them back in what looks like exactly the same hairstyle as before. "Yes? What about it?"

Cam looks like he's swallowed the sharp corner of a potato chip and it's stuck somewhere deep in his throat. "I don't know if we can save it."

Ana pauses, her whole body coming still as she considers this. "Well," she says eventually, "this doesn't seem … … the kind of conversation I want … … without really good snacks. Let's go … … for lunch. I'll drive." And she turns and walks straight out the door without stopping to check with us. I'm still in my running shirt, for crying out loud.

"Lunch?" Cam asks, shrugging at me.

"Tell Ana I need fifteen minutes." I sprint for the stairs. When I fling open the door to my room, I think for a moment that I've lost my suitcase. All I can see is the heap of bedsheets where I tossed them on the floor this morning—oh.

When I dig through the sheets, I find a pile of my unfolded clothing, and when I burrow a hand down far enough, yep. There's my suitcase, under a mound of clothing. I've been picking my outfits off the top and tossing the clean laundry back into the pile without bothering to fold anything. I mean, it's just tee shirts and shorts. Summer style. Who cares about a tiny little wrinkle here and there?

Finding something to wear to lunch, though? A little harder. I grab one of my freshly-washed church shirts and my dark-wash jean capris and sprint for the shower, tossing my hearing aids onto the counter and hoping no one knocks on the door for the next five minutes.

● ● ●

When I collapse into the passenger seat of Cam's borrowed minivan approximately fourteen minutes and fifty-nine seconds later, Ana is already strapped into the backseat, her purse tossed upside-down on the seat beside her.

"No shop talk until after we eat," she declares, and then proceeds to regale us with the various adventures (and misadventures) that encompassed her house-buying experience. "After the first date with the realtor," she says, shaking her head ruefully, "I knew I couldn't buy the house, no matter … … I liked it. I wasn't … … let *him* have my commission." She shakes her head again. I'm getting a crick in my neck from leaning over the backseat, but it's worth it.

Cam has lost the worried look, but his grin is still only at 50%, max. I know he's thinking about what she'll say when she realizes it all went to pieces when she left. But it's Ana. What's the worst that could happen?

I only need a brief flashback to last summer to know that's the wrong question to ask right now. Ana is defined by her unpredictability. In every sense of the word.

"Turn right, Cam." She leans between the front seats, gesturing. "I've never … … here, but the reviews online said … … fascinating entrées."

Cam and I exchange glances. *Fascinating* isn't usually the first word I look for in food reviews. *Delicious* is usually a better indicator. But not for Ana.

When at last we're settled at the table, Cam's leg jigging uncomfortably next to mine, his fingers clenched hard around my palm, Ana reaches for the garlic bread and looks expectantly at us.

"So." She tears off a chunk and pops it into her mouth, pink fingernails flashing. "What … … going on since I left?"

"The board decided to close the library by the end of the summer." If this conversation is a sore spot, I am ripping the Band-Aid off before Cam has a chance to stop me.

His hand closes like a vise on mine.

"But," I finish, "we've found a great way to get community buy-in and we think we can convince the board to change their minds."

Cam jumps in when I finish. "We thought we'd make these signs, sell them for just enough to cover our costs, and create enough public outrage, through newspapers and other public forums, that the board has to change their minds. Our petitions, phone calls, and emails didn't get through. We're too easy to ignore. But maybe sheer numbers will make them listen."

Ana tears off another piece of garlic bread. "There are a few board members who have wanted to close the library for a long time. People who measure a place by the square footage and monthly rent payments." She pops a piece into her mouth, chews, and swallows. "I have to be honest. I always thought they'd close it eventually."

Cam and I exchange glances.

"That's why I didn't come to visit sooner than this." Anastasia's skin is always pink, but I've never seen her turn *this* shade before. "I didn't want to see the town without it." She reaches for Cam's piece of garlic bread.

"Aren't you upset?" Cam holds it out of reach, rips it in half, and gives part to Ana.

She tilts her head to one side. "Why would I be upset? The two of … … single-handedly … … this campaign! … … brilliant!"

"Or we just try very, very hard," Cam says. He leans toward me when he says it, so I can hear ever word.

I bump his shin under the table with my toes.

Ana swats him. "Tell me about … … signs. I love signs!"

Cam explains them to her, drawing both sides out on a napkin. Ana tugs it toward herself, flips it over, and scrutinizes it with her nose almost pressed to the table.

"It's good," she says finally. "I'll buy ten. And I'll call my local newspaper tomorrow."

Cam and I exchange glances. "We haven't ordered them yet," I tell her.

"What are … … with ten lawn signs?" Cam frowns. "Put them up on Sophia's lawn?"

Ana rolls her eyes. "Of course not! I'll stick them up on random lawns all over town. Spread awareness that way. Make it something the news just *has* to cover. Maybe we can get on TV!"

She's saved from our response by the arrival of the food, which is heaped high on our plates and to be fair, does smell good.

"Okay," she says, reaching for a chicken wing. "No shop talk over … …"

Cam and I both nod, and I cast a surreptitious look at him to see whether or not he's going to pray after Ana has already started eating. He doesn't bat an eye, just reaches for a chicken wing and passes me the sweet chili sauce. Maybe he prayed in his head?

I hurl a quick *thank-you-Jesus* up to heaven and dunk my wing in sauce.

"Look," says Ana, licking her fingertips. She reminds me of a cat. "You … … too much."

"Worry," says Cam into my ear, supplying the word I lost when she wiped her mouth on her napkin.

"You're doing amazing thing. Let it work itself out now."

"And if it doesn't?" Cam's shoulders are slowly crawling up toward his ears. I want to place my hands on him and weigh him down, tug him back to earth.

"I thought we said no shop talk over lunch?" I interject, trying to steer the conversation to safer waters.

Anastasia snaps her fingers in my direction. "Absolutely right!" She mimes zipping her lips shut, taking another chicken wing. She's not looking at his face. "Relax, Cam. It'll all work out."

He sucks in a deep breath, pushes back from the table. "Excuse me … … just a moment."

"Me, too." I push my chair away from the table and trail after him, winding between tables (Why does everyone talk so *loudly* in restaurants?) until he stops in a quiet hallway by the washrooms. "Cam?"

He leans back against the wall, closes his eyes. Takes three long, deep breaths. And then he's looking at me again, and he looks... okay. "I'm okay."

I take his hand, lacing his injured fingers gingerly through mine.

"I'm okay," he repeats. "It...*bothers* me that I can't be good enough for this. But I'm okay."

"You know you don't have to earn it, right?" I whisper the words, soft as breath. "Cam? You don't have to be good enough for anything. Full-stop. Just cut yourself some slack. Please?"

He nods, giving my hand a squeeze. "I'll try."

"That's all I need."

We walk back to the table together, hand in hand. And maybe nothing is perfect—not me, or Cam, or Mike, not the library, or even this summer—but right in the midst of all the chaos, good things are still happening.

• • •

When we reach the table, Ana is deep in conversation with the waiter, so we don't have to answer any questions about where we went, or why. I cut a quick glance at Cam as he reaches for a chicken wing, and he flashes me the sign for OKAY under the table. And he really does look all right. Maybe a little more tense than normal. But definitely *okay*.

My phone vibrates in my pocket, and when I slide it out, holding the screen respectfully beneath the table, I find three unread texts from my brother.

> *I'm done at McDonald's*
> *Went well*
> *Not pressing charges*

I text back, *good*. I'm not quite sure how else to respond.

> *Where are you guys?*

Out for lunch. I nudge Cam's arm. "Where are we?"

"Colbie's," he says, reaching for another wing.

Colbie's, I text Mike. *Come join us?*

K

I lift my head and tune back into the conversation, but Cam and Ana are both happily involved with the platters of wings in front of us and for once in my life, it appears I haven't missed a thing.

"So, Ana." My plate is by far the fullest. I need to get to work if I have any hope of catching up. "What's it like living closer to Sophia?"

She practically beams, setting down her half-eaten wing to answer. "It's … … lovely. I … … Eva every afternoon when … … finishes day care. Sometimes Sophia brings … … to visit me … … library! And…" I can tell she kicks Cam under the table because he drops a chicken wing and shoots a glare at her. She giggles. "You'll … … this! I've started going to church with them on Sundays."

Cam coughs. "You did? Do you like it?"

Ana looks pleased with herself, nibbling at the last bit of meat left on the bone in her hands. I miss a word or two, but the nodding says enough.

"Huh." I can't decide if Cam's soft exhale is one of surprise or excitement. Maybe he's not sure, either—the way he's looking at Ana says he doesn't quite know what to make of her.

• ● •

A few minutes later, a slight flicker of movement by the door catches my eye. I tune back out of Cam and Anastasia's conversation—Ana wants to know why all church coffee is equally low-quality—to see Mike standing in the doorway, scanning tables.

I raise my hand to wave, and I can tell when he catches sight of me because he smiles, shoulders relaxed, and steps forward, weaving through tables to get to us. And I know it's just a restaurant that I've never been to in a town I didn't grow up in, but when he slides into the booth across from me, it feels a lot like coming home.

TWENTY

Mike

I WALK INTO MCDONALD'S IN KIND OF A DAZE, LIKE SOMEONE IS DIRECTING my movements and I'm simply obeying orders. It smells the same— like old French fries and regret. There's a sign on the counter that says SORRY, ICE CREAM MACHINE BROKEN. Typical.

I can't take my eyes off it as I approach the counter. I don't recognize the girl waiting behind the register. When I ask to speak to her manager, she just turns where she stands and hollers over her shoulder.

"Dave! Register four!"

An older man leans out from behind the fryer, sees me waiting at the counter, and muffles a sigh. Must be short-staffed today.

No flicker of recognition lights his eyes when he reaches the counter. I don't recognize him either, but that doesn't mean much. He could be a new hire. Or he could be the owner—I never met him.

He wipes his hands on his apron and glances back at the machine before turning to me. "Okay? What's up?"

"Last summer I stole some money from this place." That's it. The whole secret bottled up in one sentence. "Alex Johannssen got fired for it."

Dave blinks.

"My name is Mike Brady." I scrawl my phone number on one of the napkins lying on the counter. I could tell him about Eric, too. Except every time I think about him, I see him slamming his fist into the wall over and over again. Talking about control. And it feels…too mean. So I place the napkin on the counter and wait.

"I remember that." Dave picks up the napkin and scrutinizes it. "I remember the money. Almost a thousand dollars, wasn't it?"

I didn't realize Eric took *that* much. "I don't have a thousand dollars, sir. But I'll do what I can to pay it back."

He leans on the counter, studying me. "Not much you can do now. It's not worth the hassle. Just go home."

"I—"

"Kid," he says, not unkindly. "I'm telling you to leave it alone. Move on with your life. It's been a year. You're young. Fix yourself up and do something good with your life."

"One more thing." I clear my throat. I'm so close to being done. "The woman who got fired instead. Alex."

He turns, an eyebrow raised. "Yes?"

"She needs her record changed."

He sighs, rubbing grease-stained fingertips into his eyelids. "I'll make a note in her file. We can probably write her a better reference if she needs one."

"Thank you." This time, I turn to leave.

"Hey, kid."

I glance back.

"It's a good thing you did, coming here. It's a good start."

"It's the least I could do," I tell him before reaching for the door. And I still haven't done the hardest part. There's one person left to tell.

When I get to the car, I pull out my phone and call my mom. She picks up almost immediately. "Mike! Hi! How are you?"

I clear my throat. "Pretty good, Mom. I—"

"I'm so glad you called." She sighs. There's a rustling in the background, like she's sitting down on the couch. "No, Sara, no chocolate before we eat."

"I have something to tell you."

"Sure, honey. Anything."

And so I tell her the whole story. About school. About the internship. I even tell her an (abbreviated) version of what happened last summer, careful to include the fact that I've already resolved it on my own. As much as a mistake like mine can be resolved, anyway.

When I finish, she's quiet for a minute. "Oh, Mike." Her voice sounds thick, like she's sniffing back tears.

"I'm sorry." I feel gruff saying it. "I'm trying not to be this guy, Mom. I swear." Telling the truth feels like tearing the bandage off an open wound again and again and again. "I never meant for any of this to happen."

"I know." She sniffs. "Mike—"

"I'm going to change. I'm done making these kinds of stupid mistakes. I'm working on figuring it out."

She breathes into the other end of the phone. "I don't know what to tell you, Mike. You're too old for me to demand you come home for a grounding."

I wait for her to finish, listening to her breathing on the other end of the line.

"I just need to know…" She clears her throat. "Did we do something? Make you feel like you couldn't tell us? Did we not…" She's crying now. "…talk enough about the accident after it happened? Is that what this is all about?"

"It isn't about anything." I suck air in through my nose, trying to stay calm. "Mom. I swear. This isn't like last summer. I just didn't want to disappoint you. That's it. And I never will again."

She coughs. Or is it a laugh? "Mikey, that's an impossible promise for anyone to keep. Just telling us the truth next time would be enough."

"Then that's what I'll do."

• ● •

When I pull out of the parking lot, totally drained, Eric and I lock eyes, his car entering the lot with tires squealing, having raced through a gap in traffic I thought no one would be stupid enough to take.

When he sees me, he slams on the brakes and rolls the window down, grinning. "Mikeyyyy..." He draws out my name until I'd give anything to stop hearing it.

"Eric."

"What are you doing here?"

"I told them the truth." I jerk my thumb in the direction of the restaurant. "About the money. And Alex."

Eric's face shutters closed. He's not high today—he looks way too tired to be on drugs—which probably means he's ticked. There's a reason I only liked Eric when we were all drunk. Sober, he doesn't have a lot going for him. "Are you stupid?" He cusses me out, pounding a fist against the steering wheel.

"I left your name out of it."

Eric frowns. The side of his hand is purple, the bruise too deep to be from today. "You what?"

"Just leave me alone, okay?" A gap opens up, and I pull into it, doing a little tire-squealing of my own. If he bothers Skylar again, I'll put a stop to it. He doesn't have any power over me anymore.

And it feels good. Already, last summer is fading, like a balloon with no helium left in it. I still have questions, but with them comes the hope that someone—Skylar or maybe even Aunt Kay— might have the answers I'm looking for. I'm no longer a captive to the lies in my head. And the word *coward* no longer sears like a brand.

I pull onto the highway. I can get to Colbie's from memory if I'm coming from camp, but I need the GPS to direct me for the first few minutes. Out of habit, I flick the radio on, but the noise is distracting. For once in my life, I willingly turn the music down. I can't remember the last time I chose to keep myself company, unafraid of the power of my own thoughts.

For once, I think I like what I hear.

The GPS beeps urgently when my turn is coming up, and I follow a winding side road for a couple kilometers before Colbie's appears, surrounded by evergreen trees. The parking lot is almost full, and I have to drive up and down each row of cars before I finally find a spot at the back of the lot. I park the car, rummage for my wallet in the glove compartment, and pocket it before striding down rows of cars toward the front doors of the restaurant.

It feels dimmer inside during the middle of the day than it does at night, like one of those old-fashioned bars. I blink in the lamplight, the covered porch blocking most of the midday sun. When I catch sight of Skylar, she's grinning, one hand raised high in the air. She looks happy to see me—and today, instead of flinching away, I finally feel like I fit here.

I slide into the booth next to the blonde librarian they worked with last summer, picking a wing off the plate Skylar offers to me.

I thought last summer's car accident changed everything. But I finally know what it means to be Mike again, and I don't think Skylar ever forgot how to be Skylar. When she laughs at Cam after he drops a wing on the floor, she looks the same as she always has. Except, I think, happier.

I never expected we'd all end up here. But I'm glad we did.

EPILOGUE

IF YOU PAY A VISIT TO GOLDEN SOUND IN OCTOBER, RIGHT WHEN THE LEAVES are deciding whether or not to trade their green coats for red and orange, the first thing you'll notice are the signs.

You might see one or two staked into the ground at the edge of a farmer's field, or holding their own against a particularly strong gust of wind by a stop sign. By the time you reach the first neighborhood, you'll be curious enough to stop and read what they say. They are everywhere, after all. They must say something important.

SAVE OUR LIBRARY, reads one side of the first sign you reach, and on the other, I LOVE MY LIBRARY BECAUSE _____. The blank has been filled with a childish scrawl that reads *I like books*.

When you turn over another sign, you find that this person has written, *I study there*. Someone else says *The staff are friendly*, and the fourth sign says *I love knitting club*. You could turn over a fifth sign, but by now you're starting to get the idea.

This is a town that loves its library.

If you continue on and wander down Main Street, when the university students are all home on fall break and the high school has just finished for the day, you'll barely be able to see the storefronts past the crowds of people. You could be forgiven for thinking it's just a particularly chilly summer day right at the height of tourist season. If you're the window-shopping type, you might notice newspaper clippings featured in some of the store windows. Some are taped to the glass, some are framed, and some are held by mannikins or teddy bears. If you look closely, you'll realize that they're from more than just Golden Sound Weekly: there are clippings from newspapers in the bigger cities, too. SMALL-TOWN LIBRARY IN DANGER OF CLOSING, reads one. SMALL TOWN PROTESTS CLOSING OF COMMUNITY HUB reads another, and a third simply says LIBRARY SAVED!

But, if you're neither a window shopper nor particularly fond of crowds, you might wait until the students have all gone home to start exploring. Most storefronts flip the signs to CLOSED as early as 4 p.m., so you'd surely notice that the lights are still on in the Golden Sound Public Library.

That's strange, you might think, drawing closer. *The students are gone, and the shops are closed. Why is the library still open?*

If you lean in, pressing your nose to the glass, you'll see why. The tables and chairs, computer desks, and armchairs are full to the brimming. You count three badge-wearing librarians mingling with students, leaning over computers, and checking books out behind the desk. Who would have thought?

Behind the desk, a doorway opens, and a young couple walks out, deep in conversation. You might recognize them: the boy is fingerspelling, slowly, and the girl twists her long, red hair into a braid as she watches, her lips moving as she recognizes each handshape. They wave to the librarian behind the counter and walk toward the front door, shrugging into their coats before stepping outside.

You hover at a respectful distance, not close enough to be creepy, but just near enough to catch the tail end of their conversation.

"This has been the best fall break," says the boy, his arm wrapped around the girl's shoulders. "I'm so glad you got the week off."

The girl traces the edge of his wrist, where a watch might sit if he was wearing one. "I've been looking into universities in this area. For next year."

He beams.

Her phone rings. "It's Mike," she says, and passes the phone over.

"Hello," says the boy, tucking the phone between his ear and shoulder. "You did?" He pulls the phone away from his ear and looks at the girl. "He got into that program! For Music Education! In the States!"

She gasps. "He did?"

They stare at each other.

"He's moving again?" She sounds dismayed.

"She'll video call you later," he says into the phone before handing it back to her. "Sky, come on. This is good news."

She nods. "I know. I'll miss him. But I'm glad."

She still looks a little sad. The boy must think so, too, because he puts an arm around her again and glances up. At first you think he's caught you eavesdropping, but when he raises a hand to point, it's at something behind you, across the street. There's a sign promising COFFEE hanging from a window, and on a blustery afternoon like this one, when the light is already fading, a hot drink would sit nicely in your hands. "Let's go get coffee. I bet Alex can cheer you up with a nice pumpkin spice."

She brightens. "That might be true." They pass you on the sidewalk, offering small smiles in greeting, and you let them go. Maybe you'll get coffee tomorrow, instead. Or maybe you'll continue on your way and return another time. The sunsets are probably lovely in the summer.

What a nice town this is, you think, as you slide back into your car, which has grown cold as you explored Main Street. The type of place you wouldn't mind coming home to at the end of the day. A good place to settle down.

The boy and girl come out of the coffee shop a few minutes later, each with a coffee in one hand, the others clasped in between them. They get into a car and drive away, and after a long moment, you turn the key in the ignition and leave, too.

On to your next adventure.

AUTHOR'S NOTE

We love because he first loved us.
– 1 John 4:19

I'm deeply convinced that everything starts and ends with the love of God. If Hearing Lies impacted you in any way, it is because of Jesus, and not because of me. I pray over each one of my books, and I have asked God to use this book for His purposes and glory more times than I can count.

I hope Skylar and Mike's story meant something to you. But even more, I hope this story pointed you towards Jesus.

ACKNOWLEDGMENTS

Writing a book is absolutely a team effort. I couldn't have done it without the support of so many wonderful people:

Zayya, I could *never* have done this without you. Thank you for taking care of me during my longest writing days, for lending me your honest opinion any time I asked for it, and for giving me the pep talk I needed to get through the home stretch. And thank you for thinking of this title. I love it. And I love you.

Hannah, at this point I think they should sign your name to the front cover beside mine. Thank you for reading anything I send to you and always finding something to get excited about (even when it's not very good yet). Thank you for dropping everything to read this book just one more time when I really needed a second opinion. Thank you for loving Skylar, Cam, and Mike just as much as I do.

Thank you to my whole entire family: immediate, extended, in-laws, and more! Thank you for asking about my books, for celebrating with me, for ordering more copies than you needed to, and for calling all the bookstores within reach to ask them to stock both of my books on their shelves. I could not be more thankful. I am so blessed to have each one of you in my life.

My launch team also deserves thanks for their patience, excitement, and general willingness to dive in and support this story during the weeks and months around launch day! Thank you SO MUCH to everyone involved!

Thank you to the team at WhiteSpark Publishing. I appreciate you, and I love your heart for this company and the stories you tell!

I'd also like to generally thank anyone who took the time to encourage me, tell me that they enjoyed my books, or express excitement about the release of Hearing Lies. Your words mean more to me than you know!

Finally, thank you so much to everyone who has read *Seeing Voices* and *Hearing Lies*. It is an honor to share these stories with you.

ALSO BY OLIVIA SMIT

Skylar Brady has a plan for her life—
until a car accident changes everything.

Skylar knows exactly what she wants, and getting in a car accident the summer before twelfth grade isn't supposed to be part of the plan. Although she escapes mostly unharmed, the accident has stolen more than just her hearing from her: she's also lost the close bond she used to have with her brother.

When her parents decide to take a house-sitting job halfway across the province, it's just one more thing that isn't going according to plan. As the summer progresses, Skylar begins to gain confidence in herself, but as she tries to mend her relationship with her brother, she stumbles upon another hidden trauma. Suddenly, she's keeping as many secrets as she's struggling to uncover and creating more problems than she could ever hope to solve.

YOU MAY ALSO ENJOY

Gone Too Soon
by Melody Carlson

An icy road. A car crash.
A family changed forever.

Heart of a Royal
by Hannah Currie

Everyone wants her to be their princess...
except the ones who matter most.

Victoria Grace, the Jerkface
by S.E. Clancy

A sassy teen, a woman born before sliced
bread.
Just add boys...and homework.